jim thompson
south of heaven

James Myers Thompson was born in Anadarko, Oklahoma, in 1906. He began writing fiction at a very
young age, selling his first story to *True Detective*
when he was only fourteen. In all, Jim Thompson
wrote twenty-nine novels and two screenplays (for the
Stanley Kubrick films *The Killing* and *Paths of Glory*).
Films based on his novels include: *Coup de Torchon*
(Pop. 1280), *Serie Noir (A Hell of a Woman)*, *The Get-*
away, *The Killer Inside Me*, *The Grifters*, and *After*
Dark, My Sweet. A biography of Jim Thompson will
be published by Knopf.

Also by Jim Thompson, available from Vintage Books

After Dark, My Sweet
The Alcoholics
The Criminal
Cropper's Cabin
The Getaway
The Grifters
Heed the Thunder
A Hell of a Woman
The Killer Inside Me
Nothing More Than Murder
Now and on Earth
Pop. 1280
Recoil
Savage Night
A Swell-Looking Babe
Texas by the Tail
The Transgressors
Wild Town

south of
heaven

south of heaven

jim thompson

VINTAGE CRIME / **BLACK LIZARD**

vintage books • a division of random house, inc. • new york

First Vintage Crime/Black Lizard Edition, October 1994

Library of Congress Cataloging-in-Publication Data
Thompson, Jim, 1906–1977.
South of heaven / Jim Thompson.
p.   cm.—(Vintage crime/Black Lizard)
ISBN 0-679-74017-1
1. Natural gas pipelines—Texas—Design and construction—Fiction.
2. Gas industry—Texas—Employees—Fiction. I. Title. II. Series.
PS3539.H6733S68   1994
813′.54—dc20   94-16068   CIP

Manufactured in the United States of America

10 9 8 7 6 5 4 3 2 1

Six hundred miles southwest of Cowtown,
Where there ain't no trail or track,
Where the sun will scorch your gizzard
While the wind blows up a blizzard
And a louse looks like a lizard,
And the water's stale and brack:
There the pipeline seams the prairie,
Built by men, all wild and hairy,
Like the wolves who howl so scary
While you shiver in your sack.
—Ballad of the Big Line

south of
heaven

As dawn speared across the Far West Texas prairie, the last of the night's heavy dew fell. I sat up shivering, looking down along the twisting bed of the dried-up creek where six hundred of us were jungled up while we waited for the pipeline job to start. The line was to be one of the biggest jobs in years—all the way from out here in this high-lonely gas field to Port Arthur on the Gulf. But word of it had gone out weeks ago, and the men had been drifting in here all those weeks—jailbirds, mission stiffs, hoboes—and hardly a man-jack among 'em with more than an empty gut and the raggedy-ass clothes he wore. One of the few exceptions (and he wasn't much of one) was the guy I traveled with, Fruit Jar.

He was dozing a few feet away from me, sprawled out on the cushions of his Model-T Ford. I toed him in the ribs, jerking my foot back fast as he sat up, cursing and flailing his arms.

"Huh? Hey? Whassa matter?" He glared wildly out of his red-rimmed eyes. "Whatcha doin', Tommy?"

"Thought I'd tell you I was going into town," I said. "See if I can get us something to scoff."

He stared at me a moment longer, figuring out what I'd

said. Then, he suddenly winced and groaned and put on his smeary sun-glasses. Fruit Jar was on canned heat—about half the boes you saw out here were heat-heads. They eventually went blind from drinking it, and while they were getting that way even a very little light drove them crazy.

"You're a good boy, Tommy," he said, at last. "See if you can stem a little heat, huh?"

I said no, I wouldn't; hustling scoff grub was my limit. "You and me rubber-tramp it together, but that doesn't make me your punk."

"Aah, now, Tommy." He rubbed shaky hands over the stubble of his bloated face. "Well, maybe you can pick up a can of tin cow, huh? And maybe just about a quart of gasoline? The way I feel, a little milk and gas would make a mighty fine drink."

"No," I said.

He was still whining and begging as I walked away from him, and I decided that it was past time that we parted company. I'd be on a job soon, and I didn't owe him anything. Having a way of getting around was awfully handy out here, but I'd more than paid for any rides I'd got by changing tires and keeping the T-Ford running, and doing all the things that Fruit Jar was too drunk or lazy to do for himself.

I walked on up the creekbed toward town, stepping over and around the sleeping boes, brushing the twigs and dirt off my jeans and shirt. I was wearing a good hat, a gray city-style Stetson with the brim turned up front and back, and of course I had good stout shoes with an extra pair of soles nailed on them. That's one thing you learn when you make the big labor camps. Always wear a good hat and good shoes, so even if you don't have much in between, folks will know you're not a bum. A bo—hobo—yes, but not a bum. There's a big difference between the two.

Just around a turn in the creek bed, three boes were huddled around a little fire, warming up a can of last night's coffee grounds. I nodded to them, kind of hesitating, but they didn't nod back, and one of them took out a match and handed it to me. That's the hobo way of saying you're not welcome—that you're to start your own fire, in other words. So I kept on going, rounding another bend. And then I came up short, my mouth falling open in surprise.

He was a tall, good-looking guy in his middle-thirties, lounged back against the grassy hillside. He was drinking from a half-pint bottle of bonded whiskey, and smoking a tailor-made cigarette. And he gave a lazy grin and a wink.

"Tommy, boy," he drawled, " 'light and look at your saddle, friend."

I couldn't speak or move for a minute; I was that surprised and glad to see him. Then, my voice came out in a yell, "Four Trey! Four Trey Whitey!"

"Please, Tommy"—he winced, tapping his head. "Not so early in the morning."

I hunkered down in front of him, grinning from ear to ear. "Boy, am I ever tickled to see you!" I said. "Why, I heard you'd been killed."

"Just shot a few times, Tommy. Just cut up a little. It was the other guy that got killed."

"You figure on sitting-in here?"

"I *have* set in here, Tommy. And being reasonably sure that you'd be here, I set you in with me."

"Hey, that's great," I said. "That's sure good news, Four Trey."

"So act like it," he chuckled. "Drink up and smoke up."

He tossed me the bottle and a part-package of cigarettes. I lit up and took a long thirsty drink, and he took another bottle and another package of cigarettes from his pocket. We drank and smoked, not saying anything for a time. Just grinning and looking at each other, like old friends will when they come together.

"Yes, Tommy," he said, at last. "The sere and yellow days are gone, and the birds are about to bust their guts with singing. Briefly, the line starts hiring tomorrow, and you and I shall be working on it, and two weeks thence, with the coming of the first payday—guess what we will be doing then, Tommy."

"Now, how could I ever guess?" I laughed.

He was sitting on a bindle of work clothes, but he wore an expensive suit and shoes and a snowy white shirt—a *white* one, for Pete's sake! I was sure he was carrying a big roll, plenty to travel first-class. But he liked it this way, so here he was jungled up with six hundred other boes.

"So you've got the stroke on the gambling," I said, taking a small sip of the booze.

He nodded that he had. "The exclusive stroke, Tommy. It just happened that I knew some of the high-pressure from a drainage job in East Texas—Higby, remember him? So it's you and me alone from here to the Gulf. You on blackjack and me with the dice. Now, about your cut . . ."

"Hell," I said. "I trust you, Four Trey."

Four Trey said drily that that was nice, but spelling things out was much nicer. "Anyway, we'll make it the usual. I bank the game, and you cut twenty per cent of the take. Fair enough?"

"Fair enough," I said.

Maybe I should tell you that contractors on pipeline jobs liked to have one or two straight gamblers around. Nor did they mind if a couple of women followed the camp, as long as they were clean and didn't come into the camp-proper. It wasn't often that a woman did follow it; it just wasn't practical, you know, roughing it on her own as much as a hundred miles from the nearest town. But there were always gamblers. Pipelining is rough, hard work, seven days a week, and gambling kept the men from getting restless. It also kept them broke enough so that they weren't always jumping the job.

"What kind of a job are we getting, Four Trey?" I asked, because we would have to live in the camp, naturally, and if you lived in camp you had to work. "Are we down for timekeeping again?"

He shook his head, looking a little unhappy for the first time. "I'm afraid not, Tommy. The banks or whoever it is that's backing the job are putting in their own timekeepers."

"Well . . . you mean we're going to have to muck it?"

"Oh, no. We're certainly not going to stoop to mucking. It just wouldn't be worth it, getting our hands all calloused with those long-handled spoons."

I said I could muck it, swing a pick and shovel with any man. But I was just as pleased to be doing something else. Four Trey said that I wouldn't like the job we were going to do.

"But it was the only halfway decent thing open, Tommy.

The only job we could possibly hold, and handle our gambling."

"I don't care what it is," I said, "as long as it isn't powder monkey. I don't work with dynamite."

"Dyna's a good girl, Tommy. You can chew her up and spit her out, and she won't say a word."

"You . . ." I stared at him. "You mean, that's the job? Powder monkeyin'? You . . . you . . ." I choked up. "You think I'm goin' to powder monkey after what happened to . . . ?"

"A real good girl, Dyna is," he wheedled. "She wears lousy perfume, and you get by-God hellish headaches from it. But safe? The safest stuff in the world."

"Sure, it is! That's why the job is open, why powder monkeys get wages and a half!"

"You had me fooled, Tommy. You never struck me as being a coward."

"I'm not a coward!" I snapped. "I just don't like dynamite, and you know why I don't!"

"I know," he said softly. "But that's the way it is, kid. I'm down for powder monkey, and you're down as my helper. That's what you do or you don't do anything."

I hesitated. I took another small drink. He caught my eye, nodded slowly.

"That's it, Tommy. Dyna or depart."

"But, dammit, Four Trey . . . !"

"So what's it going to be?"

There was only one thing I could say, and I said it. He grinned approvingly and held out his hand. "That's my boy. Let's shake on it."

We shook. I looked down at my hand and saw that there was a five-dollar bill in it.

"Happy birthday, Tommy," he said.

"Oh, now, look," I said, feeling kind of embarrassed. "You didn't need to do that, Four Trey."

"Why not? A man doesn't get to be twenty-one but once in his life."

"But I'm not even sure that I am twenty-one. I think so, but I'm not sure."

"Well, now you can be sure," he said. "I say so, so you can depend on it."

"Anyway, my birthday was last week," I said. "I forgot all about it until just now."

He yawned and leaned back in the grass, making a waving motion for me to be on my way. "Go scoff, Tommy. Have some fun if you can find anything to have it with."

"Thanks," I said. "Thanks a lot, Four Trey."

"Just be sure you meet me out at the camp in the morning. Better make it around five o'clock. We'll have to hire on, and we'll be working up ahead of the ditchers and draglines. Wherever there's hard rock."

"Right," I said. "I'll be there."

He cocked his hat over his eyes and folded his hands on his stomach. Seemingly, he fell asleep at once. And I went on up the creekbed and into town.

They tell me that things haven't changed much in Far West Texas in the last forty years. It was a wild and lonely land to begin with; it had been so since the world was young. And when man had gotten what he could from it, it went back to the wildness and loneliness. Or so I'm told, at least. I can't say, of my own knowledge, having had no reason to go back that way, and maybe a few for not going back. So all I can tell you is what it was like that morning some forty years ago, when I was twenty-one or thereabouts.

The town was named after a place in Russia, as many towns in West and Far West Texas are. The geologists discovered that they were all part of the Permian Basin, which the drillers had first tapped in Russia, so they were given Russian names. Or sometimes Persian—like Iraan—since its underlying rock structure was also Permian Basin.

It, the town, wasn't like any other town you ever saw. There was no pattern to it. The streets, if you could call them streets, ran every whichway. The buildings—wooden, unpainted, wobbly-looking from the unceasing wind—seemed to have been dropped down wherever their builders took a notion. There'd be two or three huddled together in a row, kind of leaning into each other for support. Then, maybe a couple of hundred yards away, there'd be another building and, sitting cater-cornered to it by fifty or sixty feet, a half-dozen more.

All in all, the town probably covered a couple of square

miles, with perhaps a hundred buildings—cot-houses, stores, restaurants, barbershops and so on. All but three of the businesses—a general store, a restaurant and a garage—were closed down now. Many of them would go back into operation with the first payday on the pipeline, and for as long as the camp remained close to town. But right now it was as desolate a place as you'd ever see.

The wind was blowing as it always did—soughing and whining like a weary giant. Even early in the morning and with everything dew-wet, dust devils were dancing across the prairie, marching up and down the crazy-quilt streets like long lines of dirty clothes. It was very quiet, so quiet that seemingly you could have heard a sage hen drop an egg in her nest. And then way off to the southeast, coming from the direction of Matacora, the county seat, I heard the sound of a car.

It was coming on fast, and the racket told me what it was— a T-Ford with a patent gearshift and a high-speed head. You saw quite a few of them in the oilfields in the days before the Model-A and the V-8. By the time I was passing the first empty buildings, it was right behind me.

It roared past, almost hiding me and it in its dust. Then, the brakes slammed on and it skidded, ploughing up still more dust, and it backed up to where I was and stopped.

There was a big star painted on its side. The man who climbed over the door and came toward me was also wearing a star—a deputy sheriff's badge.

He was one of those square-built guys, with practically no neck and not much more forehead. His name was Bud Lassen, and I'd seen him and others like him in quite a few places out here, wherever there was a large influx of transient labor. It may sound melodramatic to call them hired guns, but that's what they were.

The local authorities weren't set up to handle large groups of men. Anyway, the locals were usually pretty nice people, and they didn't want to dirty up their reputations. So men like Bud Lassen were deputized for a few weeks or months, and they did whatever was necessary and a lot more besides. Because they *liked* giving people a hard time. They liked having the whip hand over men who were usually too over-worked and underfed to strike back.

Lassen put himself in front of me, one hand on the butt of his forty-five, the thumb of the other looped through his gun belt. He looked me over, hard-eyed, from head to foot, teetering back and forth on the heels of his boots.

At last, he said, "What's your name, bo?"

"You know my name, Bud," I said, acting a lot braver than I felt. "You sure as heck ought to know it, anyway."

"Don't be smart with me, punk!"

"The Oklahoma Construction Company," I said. "A high-line job out of Odessa. You tried to shake me and Four Trey Whitey down. Guess you were too dumb to know that Four Trey wouldn't have operated without talking things over with the sheriff."

He stared at me, the red spreading down his bull neck and up into his thick, pock-marked face. He nodded very slowly, as much as to say he remembered me all right. Which he certainly should have since I'd helped to get him run out of Odessa.

"Tommy Burwell," he said. "You sweatin' the line, Tommy?"

I said, sure. I was waiting for the line to open. "What else would I be doing out here?"

"Then pass the word, Tommy. Tell your junglebird buddies I'll just be waitin' for 'em to start some trouble in town. Tell 'em the first bastard that pulls anything will get his skull parted."

"Tell them yourself," I said. "There's six hundred of 'em jungled-up along the creek bank, and I know they'd be tickled to death to see a nice guy like you."

"And here's some more news for you," he went on, as though he hadn't heard me. "I'm signing on with the line in a few days—special guard. And what I said about startin' trouble goes double for then."

"I'm glad to hear it," I said. "You won't be wearing a badge."

His eyes flickered. I weaved and tried to step back. But his gun was already out of its holster, upraised to slam me on the side of the head. I threw my hands up to protect myself. He laughed with a grunting sound, and the gun barrel whipped into my guts.

I went down on my knees, doubled over. By the time I could straighten up, he was clear over the other side of town, stopping in front of the general store and post office.

I managed to get to my feet. I patted and rubbed the soreness a little and then I went on toward the Greek restaurant.

I'd taken a lot more than a punch in the stomach before and I reckoned I probably would again. So I wasn't particularly

13

upset by what had happened or frightened by the possibility of something worse. I didn't have enough imagination to be scared, I suppose. Enough imagination or experience. Young people just can't believe that they're ever going to die—everyone else is, but not them. They can't believe that they won't survive anything that's thrown at them.

When you're twenty-one, what you believe is that somehow you're going to be a famous ballplayer or lawyer or writer or something that will make you a million dollars, and that you'll marry a beautiful wife and live in a beautiful house, and, well, never mind. And never mind how you're going to do it. You just are, and that's that.

Still, a hard crack with a gun barrel can have a sobering effect even on a twenty-one-year-old, and mine had taken quite a little of the perkiness out of me. I took a long look at myself, trudging along in the dust, with my hat brim turned up front and back and my belly burning with before-breakfast booze. And the picture wasn't a nice one at all. There was nothing romantic or dashing about it. I was a drifter, a day laborer, a tinhorn gambler—a man wasting his life in a wasteland. That's what I was now. That's what I'd be in another twenty-one years if I lived that long, unless I started changing my ways fast.

I told myself that I would. The telling made me feel better, sort of removing the need, you know, to actually do anything.

I began to whistle, planning what I'd have for breakfast, planning how I'd spend my five dollars. Because, of course, I was going to blow it. That was what money was for, and there was always more where the first came from. Always and always.

There is no end to always when you're twenty-one.

I began to walk in time with my whistling. Sort of marching in time to it. Marching onward and upward to some vague but lofty goal. Or so I saw myself that long-ago morning.

What I was actually heading into was the big middle of the biggest mess of my thoroughly messed up life.

I suppose most of us aim a lot higher than the place we actually hit. Most of us mean to do better than we wind up doing. I know I did, anyway. In the beginning, that is.

I worked hard in school and I got better than good grades. The teachers at the consolidated high school in my native Oklahoma had pointed me toward college and put out feelers for scholarships. My grandparents—my only living kin—had done everything they could to help me, wanting for me what they had never had for themselves. Everyone was pulling for me, and I was doing plenty of pulling on my own. According to the high school yearbook, I was the student most likely to succeed. And no one could have convinced anyone that I wasn't.

Then, when I was just short of sixteen, my grandparents blew themselves up, and everything else seemed to blow up right along with them.

My grandma and grandpa, God bless them, sharecropped sixty acres of the world's sorriest land. Stab a stick down anywhere, and you'd hit rock after about eighteen inches.

They needed a new privy, and, since you couldn't dig in the rock, grandpa got half a box of dyna from the landlord's store. He was used to working with it; so was I and so was grandma. You live on a rocky farm long enough and you don't think much more of a stick of dynamite than you do of a stick of candy.

I was about a half-mile away, coming home from school, when I heard the explosion. And even that far away I could hear grandma scream. It seemed like I ran forever before I got to where she and grandpa were; and by then—well, I don't want to talk about it. I don't want to remember what they looked like. Because what it was, wasn't people.

I'm not sure how it happened. But I suppose a charge misfired on them. They waited a while, making sure that it wasn't going to explode. Then, they started to put a new cap and fuse on it. And then, then just when they were bending over it . . .

Don't tell me Dyna's a good girl, that it isn't dangerous. I know better.

As I say, I was just short of sixteen at the time of the accident; in another month, I'd have graduated from high school. But I didn't wait around to do it. I knew what happened to sixteen-year-olds who didn't have kinfolk, and I didn't want any part of it.

I went down and hid in the weeds along the railroad right-of-way. I caught the first freight train that was traveling slow enough to catch and I kept right on going.

The wheat harvest all the way to Canada. The stoop crops in California. The apples in Washington and Oregon. The potatoes in Nebraska and Idaho and Colorado. And then the oil fields and the big construction jobs through the Midwest and West and Far West. I'd made plenty of money to finish my education—college and anything else I wanted. I'd made plenty, and peed it all off.

A couple of years ago, Four Trey Whitey and I had worked almost six months steady, and, what with gambling, I came off the job with around six thousand dollars. And the Lord only knows how much Whitey had. So we went into high-livin' Dallas and got a suite at the biggest hotel in town, and then we got drunk. And stayed that way.

Just booze—no women. Whitey was impotent, I think, so it wouldn't have been polite for me to suggest women. I probably wouldn't have, anyway, since I'd been raised a strict Baptist, and when you drink like we did you don't think much about sex.

At the end of the month we were both broke, and I was having the d.t.'s. But Four Trey managed to get me into the county hospital alcoholic ward before he left town. That was his way; nice and considerate up to a point, but not taking anyone to raise. He'd work with you or go on a party with you, but he was a loner—a guy who didn't want anyone hanging on him. And he could get awfully damned sharp if you got in his way. So. . . .

So here I was again, trudging the red dust of another God-forsaken town, starting out on another job in the wilderness. And telling myself that this time it would be different, that I would be different.

I was walking past the deserted hotel when I heard the sound of voices, sort of mumbling and singing, and I stooped down and looked under the porch. Three boes were under it, sprawled around a big old-fashioned chamber pot and sipping from its contents.

I figured, correctly, that they'd stolen the pot out of the hotel and what they had in it was anti-freeze mixed with water from the Pecos. But I called to them, kidding.

"You boys getting pretty hard up drinking pee, aren't you?"

They whooped and hollered. "Best you ever tasted, Tommy. Come an' join us."

I said thanks, but I guessed not. "Bud Lassen's in town. Maybe you'd better play it kind of low."

They all said what Bud Lassen could do to himself, and what they'd do to him. "Hey, listen, Tommy. I got a new joke about pipeliners."

It wasn't new. I'd probably heard it a hundred times—a kind of dirty dialect joke. But I listened to humor them:

"Mammy, mammy! Big bunch o' pipeliners comin'!"

"Hush yo' mouf, gal! Them pipeliners screws each other an' does their own washing."

"That's rich," I said. "Very funny. Well, you boys be good."

I hurried on before they could stop me, and their singing trailed down the street.

> *Throw out the lifeline,*
> *Here comes the pipeline.*
> *Some bo is going to drag-up!*

An old Dodge panel truck was parked a couple of doors down from the Greek's restaurant. A panel truck fixed up like a housecar, with windows cut into the sides and the top knocked out and hooped over with canvas to make it higher.

The rear tire was flat, and a kid in jeans and jumper and a stocking cap was trying to pry it off the rim. He couldn't do it, because he hadn't let all the air out of it. Which made him a pretty dumb kid in my book.

I spoke to him, pointing out what he had to do. But he was hunkered down with his back to me, and his stocking cap apparently kept him from hearing. So I put my foot out and toed him in the butt.

There was a wild shriek. He rose straight up in the air, and his stocking cap flew off, and—and it wasn't a he. It was a girl.

And was she ever mad! And was she ever pretty! And was she ever built!

She was just about the teensiest little ol' girl that ever lived—short, I mean, and weighing maybe about ninety-five pounds. But the way she stretched her clothes, it was kind of a case of the parts being greater than the whole. She drew back her hand as though to slap me, and then she asked just what I thought I was doing, and just who did I think I was. And before I could answer her, she asked just what I thought I was looking at.

"Well?" she demanded, her eyes blazing. "Do you want me to take them out and show them to you? Do you, you big stupid goof!"

"Ma'am," I said. "Ma'am, I—I—"

"Or maybe you want me to take my pants down and show you my bottom," she said, adding that I seemed to like to play with it. "That's what you really want, isn't it? To get my pants down so you can kick me again!"

"Please, ma'am," I said. "I didn't know you were a girl. I mean, your back was to me and you had that stocking cap on and your jumper was hanging down over your, uh—how was I to know, anyway?"

"I'll bet! I'll just bet," she said, but she didn't sound quite so angry. "Just where is this pipeline job I've been hearing so much about?"

I told her the job wasn't going to start until tomorrow, but the beginning of it was up the river about five miles. "Come out in the street and I'll show you."

She went with me, a little stiffly, and I pointed—far, far away up the Pecos. They were just specks from here, blinking and winking as the sun hit them—the rows of sleeping and office tents, and the hundred-yard-long chow tent. But you could see a log way out there, if your eyes were used to it, and I could even identify the tractorlike generators, and the strung-out lengths of pipe—looking like matchsticks from this distance—and an antlike speck, moving here and there, which had to be the camp guard. But the girl looked up into my face, frowning suspiciously, apparently unable to see a thing.

"Are you sure you know what you're talking about?" she said. "You're not just teasing me or something?"

"I'm sure," I said. "I'll be up there working this time tomorrow."

"But"—she made a helpless gesture. "But why does the pipeline start here? What are they going to put in it?"

"Take another look," I said. "Off over this way." I pointed again, and she moved in close to me to sight along my arm. It made me feel so prickly and funny that I could hardly keep my mind on what I was saying. And it kept me from wondering about quite a few things that I might well have wondered about. For instance:

She was no tourist; she had come here, knowing what she was coming to—a girl with a purpose. Yet she apparently knew nothing at all about it. She was smart; you knew that at first glance. But her behavior, some of the things she said, were downright dumb. And that cut-down Dodge of hers was a very solid job—someone had put a lot of work and money into it. And the tires were top-of-the-line and practically new.

It was a car that would take you anywhere and out again. And do it fast. And why it had taken her here, why she should be here at all . . . ?

Well, you see? But I didn't. Not at the time.

"See off over there," I said, her black hair brushing against my face. "Do you see all those pumping jacks?—Hundreds and hundreds of them stretching off to the horizon."

She shook her head, saying rather crossly that she couldn't see a thing. I said that was natural enough, I supposed, the stuff being so old and weathered practically the same color as the landscape.

"But, anyway, that's an oil field. What used to be the largest shallow oil field in the world. It's pretty well pumped dry now, but there's more natural gas here than you'll find any place in the country."

"What are those?" She squinted. "Like matches being lighted! There! . . . There goes another one!"

21

I told her those were flambeaux. Big steel torches running up into the air to burn off the gas, so it wouldn't drift around and cause trouble.

"That's what this pipeline is about," I went on. "They'll build a big casinghead plant around here somewhere to dry out the gas and then they'll pump it down to Port Arthur."

She nodded, thanking me and drawing away again. She said she guessed she'd better get back to fixing the tire; and I said I was sure it was the valve rather than the tire and I could fix it in a minute. But why didn't we have some breakfast first?

"Well . . ." she hesitated, "I *could* use some coffee. I was driving all night, and . . . and . . . Are the restaurants very high out here?"

"Not for out here. Five to ten cents for a glass of water, and other things accordingly. But don't you worry about that," I said, taking her arm. "This is on me."

She came along without much urging. The Greek stopped us at the door, making me show my money before he would let us in. Which was reasonable enough in a town with six hundred floaters and a normal population of less than fifty. I let him see the five, and we went on back to the kitchen to wash up.

The cook was skimming a stew with a big spoon, and taking a swig now and then from a pint bottle of vanilla extract. He was lean and mean-looking, and I figured that if you looked in his pocket you would probably turn up a Wobbly card. Almost all oil-field cooks were Wobblies—members of the I.W.W. To their way of thinking, Eugene Debs was a conservative, and about the only person they had any use for was Big Bill Haywood.

They all hated the bosses; just any bosses. Most of the time they were about half-stewed on flavoring extract, which gave them belly pains and made them a lot meaner than they normally were.

"Hist," he said, jerking his head at me as I started to dipper water into the wash basin. "Don't use that goddam river water (*excuse me, lady*). Why save money for a goddam Greek capitalist (*excuse me, lady*)?"

He filled the basin with about three dollars' worth of drinking water. As we began to wash, I gave him our breakfast order—hot cakes, ham and eggs, and coffee. He said we'd get the goddam meat for free (excuse him, lady), so never mind ordering it.

"And don't hurry so goddam fast, will you? I'll fix you some scoff to take with you."

We were moving kind of carefully when we went back into the restaurant because we both had a couple of big sandwiches stuffed down inside our shirts. We ate breakfast pretty carefully, too, since the Greek kept shooting glances our way, and we'd got a lot more than our check showed. Each of us had a big slice of ham hidden under our eggs, and there was about a pound of butter under our hot cakes.

In retrospect, there doesn't seem much to have laughed about. We were cheating an honest businessman, and, if anything, we should have been ashamed of ourselves. Still, to us, a couple of youngsters come together, sharing with each other, the situation was funny as all hell. We'd quiet down for a minute and concentrate on our food. And then our eyes would meet, and that would set us to laughing all over again. We were laughing and carrying on so much that our food was cold before we'd finished it all.

Of course, the Greek caught on to what had happened, and he didn't think it was a bit funny. I figured on getting about two dollars change back from my five. But what he gave me was fifty cents. I started to argue about it, and he got all excited and red in the face and began hollering.

The cook came to the kitchen door and looked out. Then he came out, waving a meat cleaver as he headed toward the Greek. The Greek grabbed up a sawed-off baseball bat. Carol—that was the girl's name—Carol and I got the heck out of there.

I'd been right about the tire. All it needed was some pumping up and an adjustment of the valve. We worked on it together, making a job out of it, you know. Hunkered down side by side in the red dirt like kids playing at mud pies. Along toward the last, Carol turned to me just as I turned toward her, and our faces were barely an inch apart. We looked at each other, hardly breathing. Her eyes seemed to get bigger and bigger, and her mouth softer and softer. Her lips parted. They moved toward mine, and her eyes started to drift shut, and . . .

Fruit Jar drove up.

He wheeled into the curb, bouncing the Model-T's tires against it. He hollered at me, motioning for me to come over to him. I did so, taking my time about it. Wondering how he'd managed to get the heat which he was obviously full of.

"Let's have some stash, Tommy," he demanded, and I

stepped back a little to avoid his breath. "We got to get over to Matacora."

"What for?" I said.

"Because,"—he caught himself, his mouth growing crafty—"Give me the dough, Tommy. I ain't taking you if you don't."

I said I'd give him fifty cents if it would do him any good. He snatched it out of my hand, red eyes glaring at me from behind his sunglasses. "You got more than that! You and that broad were scoffing in the Greek's!"

"So?" I said.

"So where did you get the stash?"

"Where did you get it for that load of heat you're carrying?"

He let out a string of curses. He said it would be his happy ass if I ever rode with him again, and I said I wouldn't ride with him again if I was paid to.

He revved the motor, cursing. The car shot backwards, then stopped as he turned to yell at me.

"Better start walking, you cheap chiseling punk! They're hiring on in Matacora!"

He drove away fast, figuring maybe that I'd throw something at him. I watched, grinning, as he stopped at the garage gasoline pump, a couple of blocks away. He was falling for a rumor, of course, the kind that's always floating around a jungle. It didn't make any difference to me if the line was hiring in Matacora, since I already had a job nailed down, but I knew that they weren't. All the men were waiting here. What sense would it have made to have them go all the way over to Matacora, and then have to be hauled back?

Carol came up and asked if there was any trouble. I said that there wasn't a bit, and we could get back to fixing the tire.

"It's already fixed, Tommy. You know that."

"Well, yeah," I said. "I guess it is, isn't it?"

"Yes," she said. "Yes, it is, Tommy."

We looked at each other. I held out my hand and said, well, I guessed I'd better tell her good-bye. "I mean, I guess I'd better tell you," I said, "because I reckon a girl like you wouldn't want to kiss a fellow good-bye that she's just met. Right out in public, I mean."

She took my hand and squeezed it. Staring down at the ground and then slowly raising her eyes to look up into my face.

"What makes you think I'm going anywhere, Tommy?"

"What?"

"What makes you think I'm going anywhere? That I'm not staying right here."

"But . . ." I hesitated. "You mean you're meeting someone here in town? You know someone here?"

She shook her head. "I don't know anyone but you, Tommy."

"Well," I frowned. "I don't know what you'd do around town. Things will be busy for a few weeks after the pipeline camp opens up, but then they'll have to move it south to keep up with the job. So far away that the men can't make it into town."

Her head moved in a little nod, and she murmured indistinctly—about doing something around the pipeline, it sounded like. I looked down into her face, wondering why she was blushing so much.

"I'm sorry," I said. "But you sure couldn't work in the camp, Carol. They don't have jobs for women. Why, the high-pressure wouldn't let a woman set foot inside a pipeline camp."

"The high-pressure?"

"The bosses," I explained. "It's kind of a bitter joke, something the Wobblies started, I guess. You know, like the bosses are always high-pressuring the working stiffs."

"Oh," she said. "That's, uh, very interesting."

"Actually," I said, "they don't push anyone too hard. They can't. A lot of the men just aren't capable of hard work—they've been drifting, going hungry too long. And a lot more couldn't be pushed without buying yourself a broken head. They're jailbirds, chain-gang veterans, guys that would climb a tree for trouble when they could stand on the ground and have peace."

"My goodness!" Her eyes were very big and round. "Why aren't they arrested?"

"Who's going to do it?" I shrugged. "The line's a long way from civilization as a rule. It moves from county to county, through places where the population adds up to less than the pipeliners. Aside from that, the big bosses do a lot of covering-up where the law is concerned. They figure they have to, you know. Otherwise they'd lose a lot of time and the job would be held up, while the law poked around investigating and asking questions and arresting suspects, and so on."

Carol said my goodness again, or something like that. To

show she was interested, you know. I went on talking, stretching things quite a little, as you've probably guessed, to make myself look bold and brave.

Actually, there was quite a bit of law around the line. Not much of the official sort, but the kind you get from a rifle butt or a hard-ash pick handle. Judge and jury were the high-pressure, and they also carried out their own sentences. And troublemakers seldom came back for second helpings.

"Now, getting back to you, Carol," I said. "I was going to ask why. . . ."

I broke off for she was staring past me, a startled look in her eyes. I turned around to see what she was looking at.

It was Fruit Jar. He was clattering away from the garage in his T-Ford, the torn-off hose from the gas pump trailing from his tank.

I groaned, wondering just how stupid he could be to try such a stunt, getting his tank filled with gasoline and then trying to run off without paying. Where was he going to run to in an area like this? How far did he expect to get in a twelve-year-old Model-T? A car that was already bucking and stalling and trying to die on him.

The garage owner obviously wasn't worried. He was sauntering after Fruit Jar and taking his own sweet time about it. Then there was the roar of another motor, and Bud Lassen wheeled out from behind the garage.

Fruit Jar looked back over his shoulder. He tried to pour on more gas, and the car stalled and stopped. He fought with it for a moment, then threw himself out the door and started running.

Lassen shouted for him to halt—I'll have to admit that. But Fruit Jar kept on running, probably too scared to stop. So Lassen turned out on the prairie after him.

It was all over in a couple of minutes, but it seemed a lot longer than that. Fruit Jar running crazily, his smoked glasses flying off as he stumbled; Lassen zigging and zagging to follow him.

Lassen jumped out of his car, gun drawn. Fruit Jar looked around, then turned around, kind of stumble-running backwards. He tried to get his hands up, or so it seemed to me. But he tripped just then and, instead of getting them up, he made a wild grab at himself, as a falling man would.

It was all the excuse Lassen needed. He had six bullets in Fruit Jar before you could snap your fingers, and even from where I was I could see that his head was practically blown off.

By the time I got there, there was a pretty big crowd gathered. Mostly boes like me, and the rest the few people who lived in town. Someone had dropped a tow sack over Fruit Jar; the upper part of him, that is. His legs were sticking out, and the dirty soles of his feet were showing through the holes in his shoes.

"Hell," the garage owner was scowling at Bud Lassen, "that was a hell of a thing to do. Killing a man over a few lousy gallons of gas."

"I told him to halt, didn't I?" Lassen sounded a little defensive. "You all heard me tell him to halt."

"So what? You didn't need to shoot him, dammit!"

Lassen said he thought Fruit Jar was going to draw a gun on him. "It looked to me like he was reaching in his pocket. What the hell? You expect me to hold still while some thief takes potshots at me?"

There was a low murmur from the crowd. A pretty unpleasant murmur. Lassen's eyes shifted uneasily and fell on me, and he tried to work up a warm smile.

"You, Burwell. You knew this thief, didn't you? Had a pretty tough reputation, didn't he?"

"He had a reputation for getting drunk," I said. "Which hardly made him unique out here."

There were laughs. Ugly laughs. Lassen's eyes flickered angrily, but he kept on trying. "A mean vicious drunk, wasn't he, Tommy? When he got drunk he might do almost anything, right?"

"No, it isn't right," I said. "In fact, it's a damned lie and you know it."

"Why, you—!" He took a step toward me.

"The only mean vicious guy around here is you," I said. "And you don't have to get drunk to be that way."

That did it. He whipped his gun out, kind of swinging it in an arc to push the crowd back, then leveling it at me.

"Get in that car, Burwell! I'm taking you to Matacora."

"Not me, you're not," I said. "Anyway, what are you taking me in for?"

"For investigation. Now, *move!*"

"Huh-uh," I said. "I start to Matacora with you I'd never get there."

He slipped his gun, grabbing it around the trigger guard; getting ready to slam me with the barrel. "I'm telling you one more time, punk. You get in that buggy, or. . . ."

"He'll do it." Four Trey Whitey stepped between us. "He'll go with you, Lassen, and I'll go along with him."

Lassen hesitated, his tongue flicking his lips. "I don't want you, Whitey. Just Burwell."

"We'll both go," Four Trey insisted. "And we'll have a good frisk before we leave. How about it, friend? . . ." He winked at the garage owner. "Mind doing the honors?"

"You bet," said the garage owner. "You just bet I will!"

He gave us as good a frisk as I've ever seen, and I've seen plenty. Searching us from head to foot and proving in front of everyone that we weren't armed. That pretty well spoiled any little plans Lassen had. He wouldn't dare shoot us or rough us up now. Since we'd never be held in Matacora, I wondered that he'd bother to take us in at all. But he had more plans than I'd figured on.

"All right," he grunted. "You want it that way, you'll get it that way. Pile into the front seat."

We got into the front with Four Trey driving. Lassen got in behind us, his gun still drawn, and we took off for Matacora.

It was eighty-five miles away. Eighty-five miles without a filling station or a store or a house or any place where a man might get a drink of water or a bite to eat. Nothing but some of the sorriest land in the world—a desert that even a mule jackrabbit couldn't have crossed without a lunch pail and a canteen. So when we were about midway in those eighty-five miles, more than forty miles from Matacora or the town we had come from, Bud Lassen unloaded us. He forced us out of the car and drove off by himself.

It was a pretty bad spot to be in, but Four Trey winked at me and said it was no sweat. "Someone will come along, Tommy. Just relax and the time will go faster."

He jumped the ditch and stomped around in what little growth there was on the other side, making sure that it was free of any vinegarroons or centipedes or tarantulas. Then, he lay back with his hands under his head and his hat pushed over his eyes.

I went over to where he was and lay down next to him. We stayed that way for a while, the incessant Texas wind scrubbing us with hot blasts. And at last he pushed his hat back and squinted at me.

"Written any poetry lately, Tommy?"

"Nothing," I said. "I kind of got out of the habit along with eating."

"Let's have some of the old ones then. That one about the road seems appropriate under the circumstances."

I said I wasn't sure I remembered it, not all of it, and he said to give him what I remembered, then. So I did:

> I can still see that lonely grass-grown trail,
> Which clung so closely to the shambling fence,
> Sand-swept, wind-torn at every gale,
> A helpless prey to all the elements.
> Its tortuous ruts were like two treacherous bars,

So spaced to show an eye-deceiving gape,
So, while one ever struggled for the stars,
They hugged too close for actual escape.
Escape—tell me the meaning of the word.
Produce the man who's touched a star for me.
Escape is something for a bird.
A star is good to hang upon a tree . . .

"I guess that's about all I remember," I said.

Four Trey said he liked the poem very much, but it always gave him a touch of blues. "How about something a little lighter? A couple of limericks maybe."

"Well, let's see," I said. "Uh . . . oh, yeah. . . ."

Quoth Oedipus Rex to his son,
I have no objection to fun.
But yours is a marital menace.
So play games no more
In you-know-who's boudoir.
But practice up on your tennis.

"That's actually not a true limerick," I said. "But here's one that is:"

Said Prometheus chained high in the sky
Where he'd alternately shiver and fry.
While great birds of carrion
His liver made merry on,
"I'll bet they'd like Mom's apple pie."

33

Four Trey made a chuckling sound. "Go on, Tommy," he said. "How about that booze poem? The *Ode to a Load* or whatever you called it."

"Gee," I said. "Now, you *are* going back. I did that one when I was just a kid."

"Mm, I know," he said drily. "But the old things are best, Tommy. So give me what you can of it. Let me hear that grand old poem once more before I die."

I laughed. "Well, all right, if you want to punish yourself," I said and I stared in again:

> *Drink—and forgo your noxious tonics,*
> *Nor pray for cosmic reciprocity:*
> *Earth's ills for heaven's high colonics.*
> *Drink's virtue is its virtuosity.*
> *Yes, drink—or close*
> *Eyes, ears and nose*
> *To all that's hideous and heinous.*
> *Let moss grow on your phallic hose . . .*

I broke off, for Four Trey had rolled over on his side, his back to me. I waited a moment, and when he didn't say anything, I asked him what was the matter.

"You," he said, his voice coming to me a little muffled because he was speaking into the wind. "You're the matter. You know, if I was really a friend of yours, I'd kick the crap out of you."

"What?" I said. "What are you talking like that for?"

"Prometheus," he said. "Oedipus Rex. Cosmic reciprocity.

34

Goddammit . . ." He rolled over and faced me, scowling. "What kind of life is this for a kid as bright as you are? Why do you go on wasting your time, year after year? Do you think you're going to stay young forever? If you do, take a look at me."

I was surprised at his talking this way, because he just wasn't the kind to get personal, as I've said. He never liked to get too close to anyone since, naturally, that would give them the same privilege with him.

"Well," I said, finally. "I don't entirely waste my time, Four Trey. I've learned a lot about different jobs and I read a lot when I have the chance. One time I wintered in Six Sands and I read every book in the public library."

"Six Sands, hmm? That would be about eighteen volumes, if I remember the town rightly."

I laughed and said, no, they had quite a few more books than that. "But, anyway, getting back to the subject—this stuff I fool around with isn't poetry. It's doggerel. I don't know much about writing or poetry, but I know that much."

"I see. And you figure on getting able to do the real stuff by hanging around these Godforsaken labor camps?"

I said, no, I was pulling out after this pipeline job. I was going to save my money and get a start on making something out of myself. He studied me reflectively, chewing on a piece of grass stem.

"I hope you mean that, Tommy. Because you'll have the money to do it. Deal blackjack for me and save your stiff's wages, and you'll have all the money you need."

"I'm going to," I said. "That's just what I'm going to do, Four Trey."

He nodded, studying me with thoughtful eyes. "Who was the girl I saw you with today, Tommy? You seemed to be getting along real friendly."

"Oh, her," I said. "Oh, she's just a girl."

"I know she's a girl, Tommy. I don't think I've ever seen a girl that was more of a girl. In fact, she wouldn't have needed much more equipment to be two girls."

I laughed, a little uncomfortably. "Her name's Carol. I don't know her last name."

"Well, now, she must be a pretty dumb girl. What did she say when you asked her?"

"Look," I said, "I was only with her a few minutes. She had some idea of getting work around the pipeline, but I told her there wasn't anything for girls."

"Mmm? Don't you think that was rather misleading, Tommy?"

"No, I don't," I said, feeling my face redden. "Not if you're talking about what I think you are."

"That's what I'm talking about. Why else would she be in a place like this? A girl who brings a shape like that to a pipeline isn't looking for a job, Tommy. She has her office right in her pants."

"That's not a very nice thing to say," I said. "You shouldn't talk that way about a girl you don't even know. Why, I'll bet she's long gone by now. She probably wouldn't even have stopped in town if she hadn't had a flat tire."

"A flat tire, huh?" He laughed softly. "Well, she certainly didn't have anything else that was flat."

My face was really beginning to burn by then, and I was on the point of saying something very nasty. But he smiled at me in a way he had of smiling—warm and friendly and sympathetic—so I choked down the nasty words and smiled back at him. After all, why should I be so defensive about a girl I didn't even know and would never see again?

He sat up, gripping his hat brim front and rear and tilting it upward. I sat up also, unconsciously doing the same with my hat brim. I think I must have imitated him a lot without knowing that I did. I suppose every kid patterns himself after some older man, and I might have done worse.

He drew his knees up and locked his arms around them, looking off toward Matacora. Pretty soon I was doing the same thing. After a while, he shifted his gaze and spoke to me.

"You believe in God, Tommy?"

"Well, yeah, I guess so," I said. "That's the way I was raised."

"Then you believe that's heaven right up over us, so close we can almost touch it. We're just a little south of heaven, right?"

"Well," I hesitated. "I suppose you could put it that way."

"Think about it, Tommy. Think about it real hard the next time you're about to do something to screw yourself up."

He yawned and stood up. He stretched himself, then stood a little on tiptoe to peer off toward the horizon.

After a minute or so he said, "Here we go, Tommy. Here's us our ride."

It was a pipeline company car, a half-ton pickup, with a timekeeper and Higby, the chief high-pressure, in it. Trailing behind a ways was one of the company's big flatbed trucks. The car stopped, and Higby nodded to me and shook hands with Four Trey.

"Starting a new jungle?" he said. "Or were you just out for a walk or something?"

"Or something," Four Trey said. "You want to hear about it before you give us a ride?"

Higby said God forbid hearing about it at any time; he had more than enough to think about already. "You can have some hours with your ride, if you want 'em. Use you rigging up camp."

"I guess we could be persuaded," Four Trey said. "You don't have any other engagements do you, Tommy?"

I said, "Huh?" and then I said carelessly that I guess I didn't have anything scheduled that couldn't be postponed.

The timekeeper was fidgeting, tapping on the steering wheel. Higby told us to climb in the back, giving us a pursed-lip look to let us know he didn't care for the guy.

We had a fast ride into town—too fast for the road. Four Trey and I were bouncing around every step of the way, and we both took a banging from the loose tools that flew up from the truck bed. By the time we reached town, we were both of a mind to cloud up and rain all over the timekeeper.

But Higby saw how we felt, I guess, and he hustled him off on an errand in one direction and sent us in another to round up a rigging-up crew. So the guy didn't get the pasting he deserved.

We went down to the jungle and passed the word. By dusk about fifty men were piled on the big flatbed truck, sitting around its edges with their legs hanging off. Higby had hired on the cook from the Greek's restaurant, and he rode in the back of the pickup with Four Trey and me, sitting on his working-stiff's bindle and carrying his knives and cleavers in a dish towel.

As we drove out of town ahead of the truck, I looked around for Carol. But there was no sign of her or her homemade house-car. And I was relieved in a way and sort of sad in another. Sorry that I wouldn't ever be seeing her again. I'd never had much to do with girls—nothing at all, to tell the truth. It seemed a shame to be losing one, the only one I could have cared about, before I ever got to know her.

We were about a mile from camp when the truck began to honk wildly, flashing its lights. Four Trey banged on the roof of the pickup and shouted to Higby. Without slacking speed, the pickup wheeled around on the prairie, and went back to where the truck had stopped.

A man had been killed. He had been sitting near the rear of the flatbed, and apparently a wheel had caught his dangling feet, snatching him from the truck and slamming him down against the rocky earth.

Higby glanced at the body; looked quickly away with a sadly bitter curse. "Dammit to hell, anyway. Anyone know the poor devil?"

39

Someone said the man's name was Bones, but someone else said it wasn't his real name. He was just called that because he was so thin. No one knew who he was. On a pipeline hardly anyone ever knew who anyone else was. Pipeliners didn't have names or homes or families.

Higby stooped down and went through the dead man's pockets as well as he could, under the circumstances. There was nothing in them except some matches and a practically empty sack of Bull Durham. No wallet, no letters. No Social Security card, naturally, since this was before the days of Social Security.

Higby straightened, rubbing his hands against his trousers. He turned to the timekeeper, a prissy owlish-looking guy with gold-rimmed spectacles. His name was Depew, and he wore a hairline moustache and store-new khakis.

"I'll phone a report into Matacora tomorrow," Higby told him. "You can put that in your job log. Meanwhile, we'll have to get him buried."

Depew frowned importantly, pursing his lips. "We can't assume any funeral expenses, Higby. Riding on the truck was his own choice. He wouldn't have been an employee until he reached camp."

Higby stared at him wonderingly. "Why, you silly son-of-a-bitch," he said. "You stupid snotnosed bastard!" His voice was soft but it cut like a whip. "Do you know what the temperature was today? Do you know how far it is to the nearest undertaker? To the nearest public cemetery? To the nearest place where anyone gives a good goddam what happens to the body of a poor devil like this? DO YOU? WELL DO YOU, YOU STINKING LITTLE SHITBIRD?"

He yelled out the last part, almost blasting the timekeeper from his feet. Depew turned white and put a trembling hand to his mouth. He could hardly believe what was happening, I imagine. After all, he was an important man—not just *a* timekeeper but *the* timekeeper—the chief representative of the banks.

"N-now . . . now, really, Higby," he stammered. "I resent. . . ."

"Screw your resentment!" Higby snapped. "And put a mister in front of my name, hereafter! Make it loud and clear, get me?" He turned away from Depew, glanced around the circle of men until his eyes fell on us. "Four Trey, I can't order you to, but. . . ."

"You don't have to," Four Trey said. "Just give us an hour and some mucksticks, and Tommy and I'll bury him."

"Good"—Higby's smile warmed us. "I'll remember it. But won't you need some dyna?"

Four Trey said we wouldn't; we'd just look around until we found soft dirt. Higby nodded approvingly, and we got picks and shovels from the pickup. Then everyone loaded up again and drove away, leaving Four Trey and me with the body.

We poked around with the picks for a few minutes until we found a patch of rock-free prairie. Inside of a half-hour we had buried Bones or whatever his name was, mounding over the grave with rock to keep out the varmints.

Four Trey leaned on his pick resting, looking down thoughtfully at the grave, then raising his eyes to me.

"Well, Tommy. Can you think of anything appropriate to the occasion? A few nice words for a guy who probably never heard any?"

"I guess not," I said. "I heard some words said over a guy out in the Panhandle, but I can't say they were real nice."

"Let's see."

"Well, all right," I said. "Here it is:"

> *Save your breath, and hold your water.*
> *He's only gone where all of us gotter.*

Four Trey raised his brows at me. He said that he could see what I meant—whatever that meant.

We moved away from the grave, lighting up cigarettes. The soughing wind turned cool, and the moon climbed up out of a distant hedge of Spanish Bayonets, the giant cacti, and down in the Pecos bottoms a bobcat screamed in pointless fury. Far far away, yet clearly visible in the silvery moonlight, two wolves trotted up over a rise in the prairie, haunched down side by side and howled tragic complaints to the heavens.

A little shiver ran up my spine. Four Trey stomped out his cigarette butt, idly asking me how many boes I'd run into out here that I knew.

I said I thought I knew most of the six hundred. "I don't mean I know them well, but I've probably run into them on other jobs."

"Just probably, right? You'd have to talk to them a while, get close to them, before you were sure."

"Well, yeah, sure," I said. "Boes look a lot alike after they've jungled up for a while. When they get bearded out, and their clothes get ragged and dirty, it's pretty hard to tell one from another."

"Yes," Four Trey said, "yes, it is, Tommy. In other words, you might not recognize a man until you sat down next to him—on a flatbed truck, shall we say?"

"Huh?" I said. "Are you saying that . . . that . . . ?"

"Mmm, no," Four Trey hesitated. "I don't think I'd go so far as to *say* it. Merely to point out the possibility that what appeared to be an accident wasn't. Because those flatbeds were designed to carry men, and I just don't see how a man could catch his foot in the wheel."

I said I thought I could see how. If the truck went down in a rut on one side, and if the guy slid out to the edge, and if they hit a bad jolt—all at the same time, kind of. "That's a lot of ifs," I admitted. "But, well, why would anyone want to kill a bo like Bones?"

"The answer is in your question, Tommy. What was Bones like? Who was he? What was his background?" Four Trey shook his head. "Offhand, however, I'd say he was killed because he recognized someone who couldn't afford to be recognized. *If* he was killed, that is, and I'm by no means sure that he was."

I laughed a trifle nervously. "You sounded pretty sure a moment ago. Maybe you should tell Higby what you suspect."

Four Trey said firmly that he guessed he maybe shouldn't, and I shouldn't either. "I'll tell you about Frank Higby," he went on. "Frank's got a line to build. He has to eat line, sleep line, think line, and he can't be bothered with anything else. He wouldn't cover up a murder, of course, but he sure as hell wouldn't go looking for one either. And he wouldn't be exactly fond of a guy who did it for him."

I nodded and said I supposed he was right, but he made Higby sound pretty callous. Four Trey yawned and said that life was a pretty callous proposition when you got right down to it. The callousness was more subtle on the upper levels; you knifed a man by cutting off his credit or pulling a slick double-cross. Down in the dirt where we were, you simply knifed him.

He lighted another cigarette, slid a glance at me in the glow of the match. His expression changed, and he laughed softly, giving me an amiable nudge in the ribs.

"Aah, for God's sake, Tommy. I haven't got you upset, have I?"

"Oh, no, of course not," I said. "What the hell anyway?"

"What the hell?" he agreed. "We were tired and hungry and thirsty and we had some time to kill. So I've been tossing the bull around. I was just talking, understand? I didn't mean anything by it, and you aren't to think anything of it."

"Sure," I said, relieved. "You really think it was an accident, then?"

"Didn't I just say so?" he said.

"Yeah, sure," I said. But, of course, he hadn't said that at all.

A long while passed, and no one came to pick us up. Finally, we gathered up our tools and started into camp on foot. But we hadn't gone very far before Higby came roaring up the trail in the pickup. He was late because dust had clogged the car's carburetor—he blamed it on Depew's driving. He looked more tired than we felt as we rode into the camp, now lit up like a carnival with lanterns.

Higby took us to the main high-pressure tent, the only one with a floor and screens, and had us marked down for three hours' work. We got our badges at the same time, then went over to one of the long tables sitting out on the prairie—a table made out of planks laid on sawhorses—and washed with river water and laundry soap.

Everyone else had been fed some time before. The cook and his seconds and flunkeys were now busy cleaning up and doing what they could to prepare for six o'clock breakfast. Ordinarily, since they worked on straight salary instead of hourly wages, you couldn't have got a cup of coffee from 'em if you'd held a gun to their heads. But the cook knew me and he knew about us burying Bones—"a victim of capitalist brutality"—so he fixed us up fine.

Coffee with a big slug of Jamaica ginger in it (jake is almost pure alcohol). Then a whole platter of canned roast beef with hashed-brown potatoes and canned peaches and warmed-over biscuits. I ate and ate, only stopping because I was afraid of getting sick. Four Trey had finished ahead of me, so we carried our dishes back into the kitchen tent, thanked the cook and went out into the starlit night.

A heavyset old guy with a shaved head and only one arm was fussing around at the wash benches. Laying out bars of laundry soap and rinsing basins and so on. Four Trey nudged me, pointing to him.

"I see Wingy Warfield's made camp boss again."

45

"With his voice, how could he miss?" I laughed.

Being camp boss isn't nearly so important as it sounds. In fact, it isn't important at all, since it doesn't involve much but waking the stiffs in the morning and keeping the camp grounds in reasonable order. Wingy—all one-armed men are called Wingy—knew this as well as anyone, but he put on more airs than a line boss.

He saw Four Trey and me watching him and he puffed himself up and strutted over to us. "I'm givin' you fair warning," he said in a voice like a foghorn. "The first bo I catch droppin' his pants within a hundred yards of camp can go get his time!"

"We'll watch it, Wingy," Four Trey nodded soberly. "Fact is, Tommy and I are starting to blast slop pits and latrines the first thing in the morning."

"Well, all right," Wingy Warfield roared, glaring from one to the other of us. "But what I said still goes!"

He turned and strutted away, importantly. Four Trey and I lighted up cigarettes.

Warfield was a boomer—a guy who made the boom camps. There was a joke going around that the places had been named for him, like the town of Son-of-a-bitch, for example, which was nothing but one big whorehouse with an annex for gambling and which had the short-term—very short-term—reputation of being the toughest town in the world. The Rangers moved in after less than a month and chopped it to pieces with axes. When they did, they found more than a dozen bodies buried under the floors.

"Well, Tommy . . ." Four Trey squinted up at the sky, taking a deep breath of the cool clean air. "Maybe we'd better put a button on the day, hmm?"

"Maybe we had," I said. "It's been a long one."

He caught his hat brim, fore and aft, and crimped it upward. Casually, I did the same with mine. We said good night and he sauntered away, disappearing inside one of the twenty long sleeping tents. I waited until I saw which one he chose, then I entered one several tents away.

That was the way you had to operate if you wanted to get along with Four Trey Whitey. He didn't want anyone moving in on him, as the saying is, and he had some pretty funny ideas about what moving-in meant. I mean, it took a lot of territory where he was concerned, and you had to lean over backwards to avoid it.

The only other person in my tent was an old pappy guy, which is what they call any old man on a pipeline. I put him down as a crumb-boss, and I turned out to be right. A crumb, in the oil fields, is a louse. The joke is that the old men who take care of the tents are secretly the bosses of the lice, telling them who to bite and so on.

He gave me a cross, suspicious look, as old men do sometimes. Because they're afraid of you, I suppose, until you make them know they don't have to be. He said I was to pick out my cot, and be danged sure I didn't mess up any of the others. And I said, of course, I'd do just that.

"Mind if I take one back by the rear flap?" I asked. "I like lots of air."

"Well . . . ," he gave me a cautious look. "Well, I guess that'll be all right."

He actually had nothing to say about where I slept. But he was scared and old, and, well, what the hell? "It's strictly up to you," I said. "After all, you're the boss, and you've got the stroke in this tent."

He broke into a big smile. It was as nice a smile as I've ever seen, even if it didn't have any teeth in it. "Sure, it's all right!" he said. "Bunk down anywhere you want to, son, and if you need any extra blankets or anything, you just let me know!"

I went down the grassy aisle between the twin rows of cots to the rear of the tent. I stretched out on an end cot, putting my hands under my head and easing my shoes off. Lying in a bed, or rather a cot with a mattress on it, for the first time in weeks felt good. Too good. When you haven't been used to it, comfort can be uncomfortable.

After a while I sat up, and the crumb boss stopped fooling around up front, doing things that didn't need to be done, and came back to where I was. We talked; rather, he talked and I listened. I guess it had been a ling time since anyone was interested in anything he had to say, and he needed to talk. It didn't tell me much about him that I hadn't already surmised. You saw quite a few old pappy guys, and it was virtually the same story with all of them.

No homes. No families. Or none that cared what happened to them. Anywhere else, they'd have been in a poorhouse or an old folks' home, since there were no old-age pensions at the time. Out here, they could usually pick up some kind of job on the big construction projects. Nothing important, of course, nothing that required any real effort, but something that did have to be done.

They worked during the warm months, the summer and spring and fall—the only times there were jobs for them. In the winter they stayed in the bleak, God-awful oil towns. Bunking in the dingy half-canvas cot-houses—rag houses, they were called—or holing up three or four to a room in the rickety unpainted hotels. They seldom had more than enough money to barely squeak by until spring. Spring sometimes found them too old and weak to work, and they gradually starved to death. But that didn't happen very often. This was a young man's country—a country for healthy young men. There was little available in the way of medical facilities, and old men sickened easily. And when they took sick here, they died.

It wasn't much to look forward to, dying when you were too old and sick to work. But maybe living isn't either.

We said good night, the crumb boss and I. He went back up front, blew out the lantern and went to bed. And I still couldn't relax.

I took off all my clothes, and it was a little better that way with the cool breeze washing over me. But it wasn't good enough for sleep. I'd missed my bath that day, not getting down to the Pecos as I usually did, and I felt all prickly and sticky.

Finally, after a lot of tossing around, I put my shoes back on—just my shoes, nothing else—and went out the rear flap of the tent.

It was a nice night, just cool enough without being cold. The moon streamed through a canyon of clouds, painting a path across the sage and chaparral. I sauntered down it, feeling like I sometimes did at night in these far-out places. As

49

though everything was mine, the whole world, and that I was the only person in it.

I kept walking, not for any reason except that I felt like it and it was a nice night. Then, when I'd probably walked a half-mile or so, I suddenly came to a stop.

I was looking down into a wash, a draw in the prairie. An old panel truck was parked in it, a track made over into a housecar.

I stood staring at it, not at all sure of what I was seeing—that it really was Carol's. Half-thinking that I'd gone to sleep back there in the tent and that this was a dream, I closed my eyes for a moment, then opened them again.

Just as she came around the side of the truck.

She was as naked as I was, wearing nothing but her shoes. We stood looking at each other, and it all seemed perfectly natural that we should be like this. Just the two of us standing naked in our own private world. Then, she called my name softly, *"Tommy,"* and held her arms out to me.

And I went down to her.

I picked her up and kissed her, the first girl I'd ever really kissed. I carried her to the truck and lifted her inside. And climbed in after her.

Back in camp that night, again stretched out on my bunk, I thought of countless things I should have asked her. One very important thing in particular. And it seemed incredible that I'd asked her nothing at all, that we'd hardly talked at all. Yet on the other hand it seemed natural enough, exactly the way it should have been. And basically I guess it was.

We were two kids, a young man and a young woman, come together for the first time. The first time for her, yes, as well as for me. For as little as I knew about women, I knew that much. We had given each other the gift that can only be given once. And in the glory and wonder of giving it, we had no thoughts for anything else.

How could we talk at such a time? How could I even think of questioning her?

Frankly, I would have been a little worried about myself if I had.

I settled down under the blankets, contentedly tired and ready to sleep. But I wasn't due to get much that night. My eyes were just drifting shut when the beam of headlights swept the prairie—only one pair at first; then another and another and another until the landscape leaped and danced with light, and the sound of laboring motors filled the air. I opened the tent flap wide and looked out.

The cars were all the same make, big Hudson sedans. Their rebuilt bodies were half-again as long as they had been originally, and they were equipped with extra-heavy duty springs and tires. Canvas water bags hung from the radiator caps. A winch, for winching out of quicksand and mud, was bolted to the reinforced front bumper. Roped to the roof were four spare tires, and a set of digging out tools. Roped to a built-on platform at the rear was a pile of baggage.

They were stagecoaches, and they went wherever man went, to all the places where trains didn't go and never would.

Just as the horsedrawn stagecoach was the forerunner of the train, these were the forerunner of our present-day bus system. The drivers wore boots and broadbrimmed hats, and they were tanned the color of saddle leather. They wore gunbelts and .45's, and they didn't wear them for decoration.

Their passengers that night were welders and other skilled workmen—dragline and ditcher operators, heavy-machinery mechanics and the like. They were high-pay men with strong unions, so they doubtless all owned cars. Which, needless to say, they'd been smart enough to leave at home.

A pipeline was no place to bring a car, not if it was worth anything. It would be stolen—whole or piece by piece—the first time you turned your back to it.

The long line of Hudsons pulled into camp, and drove off into the night again. Their recent passengers began to bunk down in the tents, calling back and forth to each other, and making a lot of noise about it. They were sore. They had a right to be. The line had waited until the very last minute before notifying them to report to work in the morning. They were worn out from traveling, yet they would get almost no rest before facing up to a hard day. They were hungry, but they could get no food.

The pipeline company—its financial backers, rather—had let them in for this hardship merely to save a few dollars. The relatively small cost of feeding them supper. For if a man was in camp, he had to be fed.

Normally, the bosses on pipeline jobs were pretty free and easy about such things. Your wages were docked a dollar a day for room and board ("slop and flop"), and if you didn't have any pay coming—if you were in camp a day before the job started—you were welcome to eat without paying. But it obviously wasn't going to be that way here. The moneymen on this job weren't giving anything away.

Everything finally quieted down, and I went to sleep. Little more than an hour later, about an hour before dawn, I was awakened again.

Truckloads of men were coming into camp—the common working stiffs, guys who had been jungled up in town while they waited for the job to open. They climbed down from the big flatbeds, hurried bleary-eyed into the tents to claim bunks for themselves. Like the welders and other skilled workmen, they, too, were victims of the line's penny-pinching. Called into camp at the last possible moment to save the cost of one meal.

They were hungry and worn-out, too tired to do anything but curse. About as capable of doing the hard day's work that lay just ahead of them as hospital patients. So the penny-pinchers would find their stinginess a damned expensive business. And I wondered how anyone could have been so stupid. But so-called smart people often outsmart themselves, I've found.

To make a dollar, they make an enemy for life. To save a dollar, they lose a hundred. They have eyes only for what's happening at their end of the rope, overlooking the guy at the other end.

The camp never got quiet again that night, but I went to sleep anyway. An hour passed—a little less than an hour, actually—and it was dawn. And I was brought wide-awake by Wingy Warfield's foghorn voice.

"YEEOWWW!" he yelled. "YOW, YOW, YOW, YEEOWWW! Grab your shirt and hit the dirt! Yow, yow, yow! Pile out, you boes, get on your toes, an' blow your nose on your underclothes! YOW, YOW, YOW!"

Since most of the other men were already dressed, they were at the wash benches ahead of me, dabbling at their faces and hands and then running toward the long chow tent. They began to pile up at the entrance where Depew and his assistants were checking them off for time. There were sullenly restless grumbles at the delay, then yells and shouts and curses. And then they were storming into the tent from all directions, through the front and under the sideflaps. Knocking Depew and his helpers out of the way, bowling over everyone who tried to stop them.

There was a blast of gunfire. I looked up from washing. It was Bud Lassen. He was firing into the air, but not by very much. A little bit lower and he would have hit someone, and that, of course, would have been the end of him and probably the end of the camp. It would have started a riot that nothing could have stopped.

I stared at him, stunned, as he raised his gun to fire again, almost holding it level. Depew was only a few feet away, making no move at all to stop him. Actually grinning, a smugly mean little grin, as he watched. I looked around wildly for Higby, but I couldn't see him. As I learned later, he was deliberately keeping out of sight, since Depew was running this end of the show and Higby wanted no part of it.

I let out a yell, a warning, but no one heard me. There was too much noise. I yelled again and then I vaulted over the wash bench and ran. Wondering why no one but me could see the terrible danger, why they kept on jamming into the tent when they should have been running for their lives.

Bud apparently saw or sensed my approach. He hesitated for a second, then swerved the gun toward me.

He wasn't quite fast enough. His moment of hesitation had let me get in close, and I left my feet in a flying tackle, hitting him just above the knees.

He did an almost complete flipflop, came down hard on the ground, the gun flying from his hand. As he rolled and grabbed for it, I threw myself on top of him, and began to pound him in the face.

I was killing mad. Everything had piled up in me—the loss of sleep, the senseless cruelty of the line's backers, the brutal murder of Fruit Jar. All the indignities and humiliations I had suffered or felt I had suffered during my weeks of waiting for work had piled up in me, and now crashed down on top of me. Something seemed to snap in my brain, and all I could see was a red haze. And I did my damnedest to beat Bud Lassen to death. I was screaming that I would kill him when Four Trey and some other guys dragged me off of him.

I tried to break away from them, to get at him again. Four Trey shook me, yelling for me to stop for God's sake. But I wouldn't; I guess I couldn't. So he knocked me cold with a hard clip to the button.

He may have hit me a little harder than he intended. (And just maybe he didn't either!) At any rate, it was one hell of a good punch. When I came to, Four Trey was carrying me over his shoulder, lugging me down the gentle slope away from camp. I mumbled foggily, and after a few more steps he paused in a kind of natural hedge of sage brush and set me gently upon my feet.

"Okay?" He frowned into my face. "All right now?"

"Sure," I said, slurring the word. "What—where'sh ev'yone—?"

"Never mind!" he snapped. "Just stay here and keep out of trouble! Stay right here, get me?"

I nodded fuzzily, wondering why he was so sore. He turned and went back up the slope, and I rubbed the fog out of my eyes, at last coming into full consciousness.

Above me, men were streaming out of the chow tent— coming *out* of it, not going in—and the strawbosses were sorting out their crews for the day's work, then pointing them to the particular trucks they were to ride. In the distance, I heard the rocking chug-chug of the ditching machines. Still further away a chorus of jackhammers began to chatter. There were shouts, whistles, cries of "*Over here, bo!*" Then the first of the big flatbeds broke into a thunderous roar, wheeled out of camp with its jampacked load of men. One by one the others roared thunderously and followed it, a rocking jolting procession of men and machines heading for the start-o'-line.

The last of the racket died away, and the camp was almost completely silent.

Four Trey came into view, started down the slope with an armload of tools. I hurried to help him, but he pushed past me with a curt shake of his head, leaving me to trail after him empty-handed.

He dropped the tools in the growth of sage. Stood examining the terrain for a few moments. At last he turned back to me, made a sweeping gesture with one hand.

"All right," he said, "this is our latrine. Fifty feet long, three wide and two deep. Grab yourself a mattock and get busy."

I picked up a mattock—a pick with a wide blade. He went back up the slope to the supply tent, returning a few minutes later with a case of dynamite balanced on one shoulder and two steel rock drills on the other.

He dropped the drills on the tool pile, then carried the dyna some fifty feet farther before easing it down to the ground. Leaving it there, he went on another fifty feet or so to a bare place in the prairie, where he carefully took a small box of dynamite caps from his pocket and held it in both hands as he lowered it to the earth.

A dyna cap is black and not much bigger than a penny. It is the percussive force which sets off the dynamite charge and it explodes very easily, and one of them is enough to blow off a man's hand.

Coming back to where I was, Four Trey picked up a mattock and went to work with me. Neither of us saying a word as we marked off a rough outline of the latrine, then began clearing it of sage and grass. Finally, after we had been at it for more than an hour, he rested on his mattock and slanted a wryly amused glance at me.

"Getting hungry, Tommy?" he asked.

"I can make out," I said. "You don't hear me kicking, do you?"

"You should have eaten early. Machine and powder men always eat early."

He was right, of course; I should have left a call with the crumb boss. But it had been so long since I'd worked powder that I'd forgotten.

"All right," I said. "It's my own fault."

"It's not the only thing, Tommy. That brawl with Lassen was your fault, too."

"All right," I said again, but I was beginning to boil. "He was about to shoot into a crowd, and it was my fault for trying to stop him. I should have let him start a riot and have the camp torn down . . . ?"

"It's your fault for being stupid"—there was a sharp edge to his voice. "Sure, Depew is a complete stinker, but he's not a sap. Did you actually think he'd allow Bud to commit murder? That he'd just stand and watch without saying a word of protest?" Four Trey shook his head disgustedly. "Lassen was firing blanks, for God's sake! Anyone even half as bright as you are should have known that he was."

He picked up his mattock and went back to work. I did the same, feeling like two cents' worth of nothing. The mattocks went up and down, *chug-clomp, clush-clush,* and the sun began to pull sweat from me like a magnet. The silence between Four Trey and me dragged on and on, and then I brought the mattock blade down on a ten-inch centipede, cutting it in two. The two halves started to run away in different directions, and Four Trey pounded them into the ground.

58

"Ever get bitten by one of those?" he asked casually.

"No," I said. "But one clamped onto my bare leg once. I knocked him off all right, but there were these two rows of little holes like pinpricks where he'd held on with his feet. They got infected and I had chills and fever for a week."

"Is that a fact?" Four Trey shook his head interestedly. "I've been lucky, I guess. I got bit by a tarantula, but I was more scared than hurt. The biggest damned spider you ever saw, Tommy. As big around as a saucer and furred like a rabbit."

"I'll bet it jumped on you," I said, because tarantulas are great on jumping. Four Trey said I'd bet right.

"I was lighting a cigarette from a coal-oil lamp, and the thing jumped at the light. They go for light, you know. It missed the lamp and landed right across my mouth and nose."

"Holy cow!" I said. "That must have given you a jolt!"

"It did, Tommy," he chuckled. "Oh, it did. I wouldn't care to go into embarrassing details, but the hotel made me buy them a new mattress and bedclothes."

We laughed about it, the laughter almost making me forget how hot and hungry I was. Four Trey scrubbed his palms against his pants and took another grip on his mattock.

"Now, getting back to Bud Lassen, Tommy. . . ."

"Yeah?" I said, a little nervously. "What, uh, how do I stand on that, Four Trey?"

"Well, Lassen shouldn't have been firing into a crowd, blanks or no blanks. So Depew couldn't have you run out of camp like he wanted to. Higby threatened to take the matter right to the top, and Depew had to back water."

"I'm glad Higby took my part," I said. "I just wonder why he ever hired Lassen in the first place."

"He didn't. Depew hired him over Higby's head. But, Tommy . . . ," Four Trey gave me a sober look, "forget that stuff about Higby's taking your part. Don't lean on it, because he'll never do it the second time. Not unless it suits his own purposes."

"Well, sure," I said. "But . . ."

"Lassen's gone to Matacora to get himself patched up. If you'd really hurt him, instead of hurting his appearance, Higby would have had to let you go. Because he isn't going to run any real risk of losing his job on your account or anyone's. He can't, Tommy. There's just one big pipeline construction job in the world. That's this one. There's just one job open for a big-line construction superintendent, and Higby's holding it. He either works here or he doesn't work."

"Well," I hesitated. "There's always another job coming up somewhere."

"Not this kind. The only kind he knows. And there may never be another one."

Four Trey paused in swinging the mattock and wiped the sweat from his face. There was a peculiar sadness in his eyes, something I could not understand at the time, although I eventually did.

"Yes, Tommy, I think we may be near the end of an era. The building of the last big pipeline. I think we may be the first white men to come this way, and after we're gone . . ." He shook his head, resumed his grip on the mattock. "Watch yourself around Bud Lassen from now on, Tommy. Keep your guard up. Don't do anything that he can twist into trouble."

I nodded, with a twinge of uneasiness. I thought of *her*, of Carol, and I wanted to say something about her being here. But I knew what Four Trey's reply would be—and, of course, he was wrong about her! So . . . so I kept my mouth shut.

We had the latrine and garbage areas cleared of brush by noon and most of the shot-holes drilled. Since the pipeliners' noon meal was sent out to the job, we ate almost by ourselves in the big chow tent. I put away a great deal more food than I should have, and when we went back out in the sun I had to make a sudden run for the bushes. I came back out of them weak and headachy and wanting nothing so much as to go to bed, and Four Trey pointed to the sixteen-pound sledge hammer.

I picked it up. He picked up a rock drill. He jobbed it around in the rock, marking out a shot-hole, then held it upright and nodded to me. I swung the sledge, bringing it down on the head of the drill. Each time I hit it, Four Trey shook and twirled it, forcing out the ground-up rock. My sledge blows had to be timed with this, striking when he had the drill upright. And, of course, it was my job to swing the sledge.

There was a strict protocol to this. The powder monkey handles the drill, and his assistant does the heavy work. Four Trey had done a lot of things during the morning that I should have done, but I couldn't let him go on doing it. For that matter, he was obviously of no mind to, being very tired and hot himself.

We were working on the last hole when I swung the sledge out of time. Just a little, but that was enough. It grazed the head of the drill, zipped down the side where Four Trey was holding. He jerked his hands back with a howl, clutching them between his knees as he did a doubled-over dance of pain.

"Jeez-ass Kee-rist!" He glared furiously at me. "What in the name of the living God is the matter with you, Tommy?"

"I'm sorry," I mumbled. "I'm sure as hell sorry, Four Trey."

"Sorry! A hell of a lot of frigging good it does to be sorry! Just come out of your goddam daydreaming and you won't have to be sorry!"

I began to get sulky and sore and I said it was all the fault of the bosses. They should have given us a jackhammer, and we could have drilled every hole we needed in an hour. Four Trey told me to stop talking like a damned fool.

"It takes power to run a jack, doesn't it? How the hell they going to give us a generator when they need 'em on the line?"

He went on cursing and scolding me, and finally I lost my temper and started yelling back at him. "Just what the hell do you want me to do, anyway? I said I was sorry. I apologized all to hell over the place. Now what else do you want me to do?"

"I want you to snap out of it! I want you to stop acting like a Goddamned dreamy horse's ass! I . . ." He caught himself, swallowed heavily. "Sorry, Tommy," he said quietly. "It was my fault as much as yours."

"Well, no, no, it was my fault," I said. "It really was, Four Trey. But. . . ."

"Never mind," he gave me a quick grin. "Never mind, Tommy, boy. It's been a sour day, but sweet night's a-comin'. So let's shoot some powder."

We were shooting the latrine area. Part of the ground structure was soft and could be mucked without blasting. The rocky area took twenty-four shot holes, twelve on each side.

While Four Trey measured off fuse lengths and cut them with his shooter's knife, I brought down the dyna case and opened it. Then, working opposite each other, we dropped a stick of dynamite into each hole. As a rule, they went down easily until they rested on the bottom of the hole. When they didn't, we poked and tapped them down with tamping sticks.

I didn't mind this part a bit, since it takes a twelve-pound blow to explode dynamite. But that was only part of the job. We had drilled two-shot holes, which meant that another stick went on top. And that second one took the little black cap.

Four Trey began capping the sticks on his side, clamping a fuse to the top of each cap. I waited a moment, hoping ashamedly that he would cap for me also. But he stuck strictly to his own side, dropping the fuse-sticks into the holes as fast as he capped them, then tamping them down firmly whenever they required it.

He whistled softly as he worked. Not once did he look at me, seemingly taking it for granted that I was holding up my end of the job. I waited a moment or two longer, clearing my throat nervously, and he still didn't give me a look or a word. So, finally, I took a cap and a fuse and went to work.

I worked fast. A lot faster than I should have, since I wanted to get the job over with. Despite the stall I'd put up, I was finished ahead of Four Trey, and this *did* get a look from him—a long, thoughtful look. Then, lowering his eyes again, he began tying the unattached fuse ends together.

"Got 'em all tamped down good, Tommy?"

"Well, sure," I said. "Hell, yes."

"You know what could happen if you didn't."

"I got 'em in good," I said. "Real good. I mean, hell, you can check 'em yourself if you want to."

"Why, thank you, Tommy," he drawled. "Thank you very much."

He went down my line of shots, testing them with his tamping stick, occasionally bending over to examine one. I watched him, not quite sure which I was most afraid of—the blowup from the dyna or the one I'd get from him if he found something wrong. But he didn't find anything, no thanks to me. I'd been lucky, and the shots were all in tight.

"Very good, Tommy." He gave me a cocked brow look of approval. "I'll make a shooter out of you, yet."

He hunkered down, took the tied-together fuse ends in his hand. With the other hand, he struck a match to them, setting them all to burning evenly, so that the shots would all go off together. (If they didn't, a live shot might be buried under the dirt and rock.)

The twenty-four fuses sputtered; began to burn black-red toward the shot-holes. Four Trey stood up.

"Fire in the hole!" he shouted, and I echoed his cry: "*FIRE IN THE HOLE!*"

I ran, then, a good long way back into the sage. Four Trey didn't run at all. He just walked, not dragging his feet, of course, but not working up a sweat either. And he stopped before he was back even half as far as I was.

He stood facing the shot, as the day seemed to blow up around us. Tons of rock and shale soared up into the air, some of it splashing out sidewise like water from a leaky sprinkler. Big chunks of it veered toward him, began to drop down around him. But he stayed where he was, weaving a little to let it go past, sometimes batting at it with his tamping stick.

At last, everything was quiet again. The blown-up sky had sealed itself, and the air was clear of dust. We walked back to the latrine site.

Four Trey walked around it, looking it over carefully. Examining the depth of the blasts. It was all okay apparently; no buried shots. So we picked up shovels and mucked out the loose earth and rock, banking it high in front and low in the back.

It didn't take long. Not nearly as long as I would have liked. We finished with work time still left and with a job still left to do. Four Trey said we'd better get to hell at it.

It—the slop pit—was somewhat closer to camp. It had to be, since the cook and kitchen staff simply wouldn't carry slops very far. Four Trey and I worked as before, one to each side. I put my shots down as before, by-guess and by-God, and hoping for the best.

Again I finished ahead of him, but this time he didn't ask if I had the dyna down good. He didn't check the shots to see that I had. He simply fired them.

I ran. I turned to find Four Trey running with me.

The blast went off.

It wasn't like the first one. It didn't *sound* like it, somehow. And it was ragged, to use a shooter's term. A chunk of rock as big as a man's head shot right toward the rear flap of the kitchen-tent. It struck against the tent pole, almost knocking it over. There were shouts and yells from inside, and the cook stuck his head out and shook his fist at us.

Finally, the dust settled and Four Trey crooked a finger at me. I followed him to the site of the slop pit, my head hanging like a beaten dog's.

"Well, let's see," he said musingly, after he had finished his inspection. "Let's just see. I figure you laid the second stick on two of your shots practically on top of the ground. You hardly tamped them down at all. So that means. . . . Can you tell me what it means, Tommy, boy?"

I nodded miserably, unable to meet his eyes. "Yeah, I guess I do, Four Trey. I guess so."

"Guess, Tommy? You don't guess with dyna—not more than once."

"All right!" I said. "All right, damn you! It means I've got two sticks of dynamite buried under the rubble!"

"And, Tommy? And? I suppose you expect me to dig them out for you?"

"I don't expect anything such of a damned thing!" I said. "I wouldn't let you do it for all the tumblebugs in Texas! I'm going to do it myself, so you just get the hell back out of the way!"

He did, and I did. When I found the buried shots, I clamped caps and fuses on them and blew them. And I acted like he did when he shot powder. I stayed in fairly close, weaving my body to dodge the fill, even batting at a little clod of dirt with my hand when it sailed close to me.

That one little clod was all that did come close. With only two one-stick shots and both of them deep, I was in no danger at all. None from flying rock, that is. There'd been plenty of danger in digging out the shots.

Four Trey and I scooped the pit out and banked it. Then, our day's work was done. The men hadn't come in from the line yet, but their time began when they got there and ours started here.

We gathered up our tools and equipment and checked them in at the supply tent. At the wash benches we stripped and took baths, taking turns at pouring pails of water over each other. All this in silence. Neither of us said anything, even when Wingy Warfield started yelling about us wasting water.

Wingy wandered away, mumbling to himself. Four Trey and I finished washing and got dressed again. Our eyes met, and I tried to look stern and haughty; just why I don't know. But somehow everything suddenly struck me ridiculous, and I almost broke into laughter.

Four Trey gave me a deadpan look, but his eyes were twinkling. "Something on your mind, Tommy?" he asked.

"N-No, no," I said. "No, I j-just—*ha, ha*—I was just—*ha, ha, ha*. . . ."

And then I doubled up laughing, whooping and hollering and wheezing like nine kinds of a damned fool. I laughed and laughed, while Four Trey looked on, grinning and nodding as if I were doing exactly what I should have. And maybe I was, I guess, because it seemed to straighten out an awful lot of things inside me and to put me into perspective with myself. Without quite knowing that I was doing it, I could see Tommy Burwell as he was and accept him: his fears, his pretentiousness, his preposterous strutting and posing, his bad as well as his good. Without knowing that I was doing it, I met maturity and accepted it.

I washed my face again, washing away the tears of laughter. Four Trey gave me a full dipper from the drinking-water barrel, and we lighted up cigarettes. He crimped up his hat brim, fore and aft, and I did the same with mine. So we stood there smoking and talking quietly and sniffing the good smells of supper; man and boy—man and *man*—late in the afternoon of the Far West Texas day. The sage suddenly turned golden; the shortgrass, perpetually leaning with the wind, seemed abruptly to catch fire.

Out on the line, the chattering of the jackhammers came to a stop, and the ditcher gasped a final *chug-whush* and was silent. One by one, the firm throbbing of the generators dwindled into sobs, growing weaker with lengthening distance between them until they were gone entirely. For a brief space, then, there was nothing, no sound at all—an immeasurable hiatus of silence, a tiny void in a universe of noise. Then there was the hail of a man's voice, reedily thin with distance but coming clear in the clean air. *"Eeeyahoo!"* Then another hail and another, hundreds of them doubtless, smothering and mingling with the racket of muck sticks dropped and flung aside. And then the big flatbeds began their barking roar, hogging out all other sound but their own, thundering and fuming and groaning.

The first day's work was over. The men were coming in from the line.

The welders and machine men rode the first truck. This was protocol; the best men got the best, were entitled to first place, and I never heard anyone complain about it. The succeeding trucks carried the common working stiffs, seated around the outside edges of the flatbeds or squeezed squatting in the inside. The truck swampers stood on the running boards, while the strawbosses rode with the truck-drivers. This, too, was accepted protocol; a strawboss outranked a swamper and was entitled to preempt him.

The machine men, the welders and strawbosses were hungry and exhausted—who wasn't?—but there was something in their expressions, the way they carried themselves, which drew a sharp line between them and the working stiffs. Quite likely, they were even more tired than the working stiffs, since their jobs demanded more of them and it was impossible for them to dog it as a muck-stick artist could. But still they didn't look as tired; they didn't show it as much. They had come from somewhere, not nowhere, and they were going somewhere, not nowhere. They had something to live for, in other words, something to look back on. And having it put starch in their spines; it gave them a look that you could note without being made uneasy, without wondering uneasily whether you looked the same way and hoping to God that you never did.

As for the working stiffs. . . .

They climbed down from the flatbeds, and every bit of their weariness and hunger was apparent; this day's and all the bitter days before this. All the emptiness of all those days and all the days that lay ahead of them. And the bad part about it was that they didn't seem to mind. They had got through a day. Getting through a day, getting through it any way they could, was the sum total of their lives. Worn out as they were, they did a lot of joking and laughing. *Why not, anyway?* They laughed at all the things they should not have laughed about. At their general worthlessness, the filthiness of their clothes and bodies—clinging with mud made of mingled dust and sweat.

Their ancient garments had given way under the strain of their first day's work. Pants showed great rips, with dirty flesh peeking through. Shirts had split into shreds, and many had been discarded, the men going naked from the waist up. Headkerchiefs instead of hats were common, dirty bandannas tied around the head pirate-style.

Most of the men made a stab at washing, but it was something they didn't have to do so they didn't do much of a job of it. The general effect was of smearing the dirt around instead of getting rid of it.

I wondered how I could have been around these men for

weeks while waiting for the job to open without realizing how terrible they truly were. How I could have put up with them for even a day. But I suppose it was because I had been out of work so long, because I had lacked better men to compare them with.

Four Trey gave me a little nudge, pointed to the entrance flap of the chow tent, where the welders and other skilled workmen were already gathering.

"We better get up there, Tommy."

"Yeah," I said, "we sure as heck had," and we did.

The eating-early privilege didn't apply at night. Actually it wasn't a privilege, being more a means of speeding up the work. At night, it was more convenient for everyone to eat at once—more convenient for the pipeline, that is—so everyone did.

There was a mob behind us by the time supper was served. It swept us forward, carrying us almost all the way back to the end of the tent before the pressure eased off and we were able to sit down.

Pipelines always fed good and this was no exception. The keynote was plenty—plenty of variety and plenty of it. There were at least two kinds of everything, all served family style; two kinds of meat, potatoes and beans, and three of green vegetables. There was pie, cake, cookies and doughnuts. There were pitchers of tea, coffee and milk. We drank from metal pint bowls, instead of cups, and the "plates" were big metal trays.

All through the meal, flunkies were running back and forth from the kitchen, carrying in food and carrying out empty dishes. At the end of the meal, boxes of apples and oranges were set at the entrance to the tent, and everyone was allowed to take one of each.

Four Trey and I went out together, helping ourselves to fruit. I remarked that the chow was up to standard, so maybe the line's backers wouldn't turn out to be so chinchy after all. Four Trey shrugged.

"They have to feel good. The men would be dragging-up right and left if they didn't."

"A lot of 'em will drag-up, anyway," I said. "Some will quit in the morning, as soon as they've scoffed, and there'll probably be fifty by the end of the week. I wonder why that is, Four Trey?"

"Do you?" he said.

"Well, yeah. Here they've finally made a job, and they need dough so bad it hurts. But they blow-up or drag-up over a bad cup of coffee or for no damned reason at all."

"Mmm, strange isn't it? Of course," Four Trey drawled, "I've never done anything like that myself, have you, Tommy? We're known far and wide as the old reliables of the oil fields."

I laughed sheepishly. "Well, all right," I said. "But it's sure going to be different this time."

"It can be, Tommy," he said softly. "It can be. We're just south of heaven, remember, and if you reach hard enough and high enough you're going to make it."

"I'm going to," I said. "You just watch and see. I'm going to stay on the job and keep out of trouble and I'll deal blackjack for you and. . . ."

He yawned openly, cutting me off; it was a way of telling me something. That he liked me, but that was it. That what

Tommy Burwell did was strictly Tommy Burwell's business, and what Four Trey Whiteside did was his, and he wanted to keep it that way.

I wasn't offended, but maybe I was just a little hurt. He'd drawn back from me on other occasions, when he'd felt himself drawn too close. But I'd felt that a change had taken place today, that a bond had somehow sprung up between us, and so I was maybe a little hurt by his rebuff.

"Well . . . ," I yawned even wider than he had. "Guess I'll go sack up. Take it easy, Four Trey."

"See you in the morning," he nodded.

I started for my tent, crimping my hat brim front and back before he could do it and walking like I was in one heck of a hurry to get to bed.

"Tommy. . . ."

"Yeah?" I whirled back around. "Yeah, Four Trey?"

"Tommy. . . ." He bit his lip, took an uncertain step or two toward me. "I just wanted to tell you that . . . that. . . . Nothing," he said curtly. "I mean, be sure and leave a call with the crumb boss. We don't want another screw-up in the morning."

"Got you," I said. And then I went on to my tent and he went to his.

The old guy I'd talked to the night before, the crumb boss, was sitting on my bunk to hold it for me. I thanked him and gave him my morning call, then sat down and began to undress. All the other bunks had guys sitting or lying on them, smoking or sleeping or getting ready to sleep. Hardly anyone talked with anyone else. If they were awake, they lay with their eyes open, staring vacantly up at the canvas roof, or else they sat on the edge of their sack, staring vacantly down at the dirt floor. Seeing nothing, I guess. Seeing everything.

Up near the front of the tent, a guy was twanging on a juice-harp, playing the same thing over and over, the opening bars of *Home, Sweet Home*. He must have played it umpteen times, and I was about to yell at him, but another guy beat me to it.

"Knock that off, you son-of-a-bitch!"

Then a dozen other guys were yelling, threatening to make him eat the juice-harp if he played it one more time. So he knocked it off, getting under the covers fast, and everyone else sacked up, too. The crumb boss dimmed the lantern hung from the ridge pole. Ten minutes later he blew it out. I waited a while longer, measuring the time by counting to a hundred by fives. Then, when everyone seemed asleep and darkness had settled in, I dressed and went out the back flap of the tent.

Clouds hung over the moon, and there was hardly any light at all. It was hard walking that way, dangerous walking in view of all the snakes and poisonous pests in the area. But I got to where she was with nothing worse than a few snags from the sage. I got to where her homemade housecar was parked, down in a little dip in the prairie.

She was sitting on a packing box outside the car. Her back was to me, and inside a protective rim of rocks she had a low fire going. For light rather than heat, I guess, since the night was only pleasantly cool.

I whistled softly, so as not to startle her. She didn't seem to hear me, and I was about to whistle again when I heard the soft sound of her weeping. It sounded so lonely, so lost and frightened that tears came into my own eyes, and I had to gulp down a lump in my throat. Then I ran down the slope calling to her, holding out my arms. And I must have scared her out of her wits for a moment, but then she recognized my voice and came running to me like a child.

"My gosh, honey!"—I held her in my arms, petting and comforting her. "What were you crying about? Who hurt you, baby? You just tell me and. . . ."

"Nothing, no one." She clung to me, heaving a great shuddery sigh. "Just hold me tight, Tommy. Just hold me tight."

"Well, sure I will," I said, stroking her hair, kissing it over and over. "But, look, Carol. . . ."

"No, don't talk, Tommy. Just hold me."

I held her. We held each other close. Minutes passed, and then she lifted her face and looked up at me.

"All right, Tommy. I'm all right now, darling."

"What were you crying about?" I said.

"N-nothing. No, really I wasn't. I was just lonesome and I thought that, well, I'd never see you again. That you wouldn't want to see me again after . . . you know . . . last night. So. . . ."

I said, "Why wouldn't I? Why wouldn't I want to see you, for Pete's sake? I. . . ."

I broke off, peering into her face. She tried to draw back, but I had already seen it. A big black-and-blue bruise, puffily clotted with blood and extending from her left cheek to her eye.

"Who did that?" I said. "Who hit you, Carol?"

"No one. No, really, I mean it, Tommy," she said firmly. "I . . . well, I was fixing dinner and I turned around and

75

banged into the car door. It was standing open, you know, and I hit myself on the edge of it."

"Well . . ." I studied her carefully. "If you're sure. . . ."

"Does it look very awful, Tommy? Huh?"

"Well, it looks pretty bad," I said. "I figure you're going to get a shiner out of it."

"Then, I'll bet you don't want to kiss me, do you? Just because I bumped into a door and got a bruise on my face an' . . . an' everything, you don't love me anymore!"

She flounced around, play-pouting, turning her back to me. I laughed and started to pull her back around again. But the mite of suspicion in my mind moved me to do something else.

Raising my hand, I gave her a sharp slap on the back.

She let out a scream. Then she whirled and slapped me in the face.

"I'm sunburned, damn you! I was going without a shirt today and I got a bad sunburn!"

"I'm sorry," I said. "I just thought that. . . ."

"I know what you thought and I told you about sixteen times you were wrong! Now, if you're going to keep on acting stupid, you can just go on back to your stupid camp and stay there!"

Well. . . .

I apologized. I promised not to be suspicious any more. I assured her that the bruise made her more beautiful than ever and that I thought she'd look wonderful with a shiner, even two of 'em. I told her—well, I don't remember it all, but it was enough, I guess. Because she came into my arms again, and pretty soon afterward I whispered in her ear, and she hesitated a split second, then whispered back that, yes, it was kind of cold outside.

I lifted her up and put her in the truck. I climbed in after her, then reached out and closed the swinging doors. Just before they swung shut the moon cleared for a moment. And in its dimly briefly glow I saw a tall shadow standing at the crest of the rise. It was gone almost before I saw it—in the blink of a fast-blinking eye. So fast that I could not be absolutely sure that I had seen it or that the light and my imagination had not exaggerated its size.

I closed and locked the doors, telling myself that it must have been a rabbit. After all, some of those mule jacks stood almost four feet high, and when you saw them in faint moonlight . . .

Carol's urgent whisper came to me in the darkness: What was I waiting for, for heaven's sake? I undressed hastily and went to her, and for a long time I had thoughts for nothing else.

"No, Tommy, no! Now, you promised not to!"

"You mean you won't even tell me your name? Your full name?"

"Oh. Well, it's Long. Carol Long."

"What . . . where are your folks, Carol?"

"Parents?" She shook her head. "I don't have any."

"No close kin at all?"

Her hair brushed my face as she shook her head again. Then, bitterly, "At least I hope they're not mine."

"How do you mean?"

"Just the people who've taken care of me since I was a little girl. As far back as I can remember."

"You don't sound like you like them much."

"I don't like a lot of things! Like people who keep asking questions after they've promised not to!"

"Why are you following a pipeline camp, Carol?"

Silence.

"There's only one reason why you would follow it. Why any woman would."

Silence.

"Is that how . . . ? Did someone come over here from the camp and beat you up?"

Silence.

"No, it couldn't be. Even if they knew you were here. Maybe on payday—on payday, sure. But no one would be looking for a woman before then."

Silence.

"Why, Carol? Oh, my gosh, honey, why? How could you? I love you! You're the only girl I've ever loved or ever will! So how . . . why . . . ?"

Silence, still. And her lips stiff, unrelenting, under mine. But I felt the damp of tears upon her cheeks.

"I won't let you do it, Carol. By God, if I catch anyone even coming near you—!"

I grabbed her and shook her in a fury of frustration. I told her I ought to turn her over my knee and paddle the butt right off her.

"Why, doggone it, damn you, anyway! The idea of a nice girl like you turning herself into a damned filthy whore! Why . . . why, dammit to hell, I. . . ."

She rolled over on her stomach, and buried her face in her arms. I raised my hand to give her a hard sock on the bottom. But she started crying, and I couldn't stand that. So I wound up by kissing and petting her instead.

She snuggled against me contentedly, sighed on a drowsy note.

"Mmm, this is nice, isn't it, Tommy? Don't you wish we could just stay this way forever?"

"Fat chance," I grumbled. "Dammit, Carol, how can you. . . ."

"D-Don't, Tommy. Please, don't. Anyway, it'll be a long long time yet, an'. . . ."

"The hell it will be! Payday's a day less than two weeks off, and. . . ."

"But . . . But maybe something'll happen. Maybe it'll be longer than that, and. . . . Anyway, let's don't talk about it. Not now, darling. Not now."

"What do you mean, maybe something'll happen? Payday comes every two weeks, and when it does. . . ."

"Oh, why don't you shut up!" she exploded. "Why don't you just go on back to camp and go to bed?"

"All right, I will!" I said, and I got up and began to dress. "And I'm not coming back either! I got no use for whores, and that includes you!"

She started crying again. I told her she might as well knock it off, because I was leaving and I wasn't coming back. "I've got just one thing more to say to you," I said, hopping around on one foot to get my sock on. "If I had my way I'd—*yow!*"

I sat down on the floor hard, clutching my big toe. Carol jumped up, and somehow found me in the darkness. Flung her arms around me protectively.

"T-Tommy . . . what's the matter, darling?"

"Nothing," I said. "I just stubbed my big toe."

"Oh, you poor baby, you!" She hugged my head to her breast. "Want me to kiss it an' make it well?"

I said, "Aw, naw, it's all right," feeling kind of embarrassed, you know.

"I think I'd better kiss it," she said firmly. "You can't take chances with stubbed toes."

"Naw, now, don't," I said. "Now, dammit, Carol! Of all the doggone crazy girls . . . !"

"Let me kiss your toe, Tommy. I'll tickle you if you don't."

I tried to pull away from her. I told her she'd better knock off the nuttiness, because I was plenty sore at her already, and it wasn't going to change anything.

She began to tickle me. I tickled her.

We wrestled all over the floor, laughing and acting the fool and knocking things over until we'd practically torn the place apart. After a while we got back in bed.

I left for camp an hour later, after promising to come back the next night. She wouldn't let me go until I did, and of course I wanted to, anyway.

Camp was dark except for a couple of lanterns, one hung near the drinking-water barrel and another spotted in the area where the flatbeds were parked. I was thirsty after all my activity, so I went between my tent and the adjoining one and dippered up a drink.

I rolled a smidgin of water around in my mouth, spat it

out on the grass. I took a swallow, then another, drinking
slow because I was hot and a man could get sick from gulping
water when he was hot. I emptied the dipper a swallow at a
time, hung it back over the rim of the barrel and turned to
go to my tent.

And there was Bud Lassen. I almost piled into him.

I froze for a second, then jumped backward raising my
fists. He gestured frantically, holding his hands palm outward
in an appeal for peace.

"Don't, Tommy! I just. . . . Where you been, anyway?"

"None of your damned business," I said.

"Well, sure, sure, it ain't. I mean, I was just looking for
you, and you weren't flopped, so, uh, naturally I asked where
you'd been."

I began to relax. He certainly didn't look like he wanted
any trouble. Judging by his swollen eye and mouth and the
court-plaster strips across his nose and forehead, he'd had all
the trouble he wanted.

"I was restless so I took a walk," I said. "What are you
doing up?"

"Well, that's kind of my job, you know, Tommy. To sort
of mosey around and keep an eye on things."

I pointed out that there was nothing around camp at night
to keep an eye on and that an armed guard walked the line.
He agreed with an ingratiating smirk.

"But you know how I am, Tommy. I like to be on my toes.
I got to keep my hand in, you know."

"I know," I said. "You like to go poking your nose in all
over the map, whether you've got any business there or not.
Now, what do you want with me?"

His face tightened; for a split second, pure murder gleamed in his eyes. Then he worked the smile back into place.

"Well, you know, Tommy. Just to let you know that I don't hold no hard feelings and to make sure you don't. . . . I mean, we're all here together, workin' and livin' together, an'. . . ."

"No, we're not," I said. "I'm not living with you and I'm not working with you. There's no reason why we should have to come near each other in a camp this size."

"Now, Tommy. . . ." He squirmed. "I'm trying to do the right thing here, an' you sure ain't makin' it easy. Sounds like you just don't want to be friends, no matter what."

He was right about that, of course. But I'd promised Four Trey to stay out of trouble, and it's never smart to hold a man in a corner when he's trying to get out. So I nodded and took a softer tone with him.

"Okay, Bud," I said. "If you're saying you don't want trouble from me, I'll promise you won't get any unless you start it. Now, why don't we leave it at that and turn in?"

"Swell, Tommy, swell," he burbled eagerly. "I mean maybe I done a wrong thing or two, an' maybe you did. But now we're even, an' . . . shake on it, huh?"

He stuck out his hand. I nodded and walked past him and when I glanced back from the entrance flap of my tent, he was still standing there, his hand half-extended. He dropped it, gave it a rub against his pants and walked away. I went on into my tent, and got into bed, wondering what had come over the guy.

It could be that he was afraid of getting canned, after seeing Depew play second-stroke to Higby. Or it could be that he wanted to get my guard down before he laid it into me hard.

Or it could be both. As I saw it, however, I could be pretty damned sure of a couple of things:

That Bud Lassen's friendliness was strictly an act and that he was going to make plenty of trouble for me.

And I was right.

Or at least half-right. Whether I was any more than that, I'm still not sure.

The camp had to be pitched in a certain place: a large reasonably level area, which would be convenient to the job. It *had* to be in a place like that, and if the soil was rocky it had to be put up with. The route of the pipeline itself, however, had been surveyed to skirt as much rock as possible. And it was being dug in what the geologists call a "fault"— a place where the rock has shifted and broken. There were two downward sloping ledges of rock with a filled-in valley of earth between them; and the valley was the route of the line.

There were stretches and patches of rocky outcrop in the valley's earth, and there were stretches where the two ledges ran together. Wherever rock occurred, Four Trey and I and, of course, the jackhammer men had work to do.

Our first day on the line, there wasn't enough rock to require both a powder monkey and a helper. Or so Higby said, as we started to board the first truck going out.

"I figure you can shoot it all, Four Trey. In a day or two, of course, you'll need Tommy again."

I wanted to know what I was going to do in that day or two, but Four Trey cut in on me. "I'll tell you, Frank," he said. "Tommy's a little rusty on shooting; you know how a man gets when he doesn't keep his hand in. I'd like to get him broken in good now that we've made a start."

"I'd like a lot of things," Higby said curtly. "But—all right, I can let you keep him this morning. No longer."

Four Trey said a morning wasn't enough, and Higby said it would have to be. "You run a jackhammer, Tommy? We've got more jackhammer work than we've got men for it."

"Well . . ." I hesitated reluctantly. "I wouldn't exactly call myself a jackhammer man, but. . . ."

"Mmm. Would you call yourself a mormon-board man? Or a dope-pouring man?"

"*Huh?*" I said. "What do you mean?"

"I mean you've got a choice. Mormon board, dope or jackhammer."

"Come to think of it," I said. "I'm one of the best damned jackhammer men in Texas."

And Higby grinned tightly, and Four Trey chuckled. And then he and I climbed aboard the flatbed.

It pulled out of camp and went jolting southward across the prairie. After about a mile we came to the beginning of the ditch, and from then on we stopped repeatedly to drop off men and equipment. As we proceeded down the line, the dope (asphalt) boiler behind us was fired up, sending acrid smoke into the sunny sky. Then, the power generators began to chug and hum, and the welders' torches bounced showers of sparks from the joints of line pipe. And, then, finally, the ditching machine began its groaning, shaking clatter.

It took one man working full-time to keep the ditcher's thousands of nuts and bolts tight. Otherwise, it would have fallen apart from its constant rocking and shaking.

Only the jackhammer men were left on the truck when Four Trey and I unloaded. While we set up for work, they were taken on up the route of the line—ahead of ditch—about a quarter of a mile. They cut in their air generator, and their jackhammers began to rattle and clatter against the rock. Four Trey gave me a commiserating look.

"Too bad you got stuck on that, Tommy. Of course, it'll only be for a day or so."

"Sure," I said. "Anyway, I'd a lot rather do it than dope pipe or pull a mormon board."

"Who wouldn't? Maybe it's all for the best, Tommy. After running a jackhammer, shooting powder will look pretty good to you."

"Yeah," I said, although nothing was ever going to make me like to work dynamite. "Sure, it will."

Shooting line-ditch was a different proposition from the pit work we'd done in camp. Because the shots might be stretched out over a considerable distance, there was no cutting fuses the same length and tying the ends together; that would take too much time and fuse. Instead, you cut a long fuse for the first shot in your series (the length depending on how many shots you had to fire) and you cut the last one short. Then you ran down the line of shots, lighting them from a cigar butt (you were issued cigars by Supply) until the last one was lit. And then you ran to beat hell.

If you gauged things right, all the shots went off simultaneously and you were safely out of the way when they did. If you didn't do it right, you were in trouble. Live shots could get buried. They weren't the only thing, either, if you know what I mean.

Of course, there are better ways now of firing dynamite. Probably there were better ways then. But that was the quickest and cheapest way, so that was the way it was done.

It was an easy morning for me. The work was, at least. There were no long series of shots. Even shooting them all, with Four Trey supervising, I still hardly worked up a sweat— either from nerves or effort.

Somehow, though, I didn't feel too good, either mentally or physically. I'd missed a lot of sleep the night before, after being up most of the previous night, and the loss was catching up with me. Being tired, I couldn't fight off the black thoughts which kept creeping into my mind. Sickening thoughts about what she was going to do—or had said she was going to do. *Why would she say so if she wasn't?* I thought of her painfully bruised face—*how could she have done that by banging into a door?* I thought of her being alone and helpless in this Godawful wilderness. I thought of the tall shadow I'd seen from the door of her housecar—and I thought maybe it was a mule jackrabbit, but what if it wasn't?

Just before noon a flatbed truck stopped at one of the main workgangs behind us, and the driver and swamper set off their dinner for them. After it had gone on by us to take grub to the jackhammer men, I blew my last series of shots, and Four Trey checked them out as okay.

It was noon by then, and we sauntered back to where the main gang was starting to eat.

"You're coming right along, Tommy," he told me. "Shooting like an old pro. Getting over your scares, are you?"

"Yeah, I guess so," I said.

"I'm glad to hear it," he said. "I had the impression at times that you weren't scared because you just weren't thinking about what you were doing. If that's the case, you've been a very lucky boy this morning and you'd better not count on your luck holding."

I mumbled something about just being tired, I guessed. Four Trey said sharply that I'd better get over it, then, and get over it fast.

"I mean that, Tommy. I like you, but not nearly enough to let you blow me up. Now, if you've got something on your mind, let's get it to hell unloaded right now."

"Well," I swallowed guiltily. "I, uh. . . ."

"Yes?"

"Well, to tell you the truth," I said, and it was partly the truth. "I've been thinking about that guy Bones. You know, the one that fell off the truck—only you said maybe he didn't fall off, that someone murdered him. . . ."

"Oh, for God's sake!" Four Trey stopped dead in his tracks. "You mean you're still thinking about that? But I told you I was just making talk! Just killing time."

"Yeah, I know," I said. "But I still can't get it out of my mind. It's so logical, you know, when you stop to think about it. It could have happened just the way you said. . . ."

"A lot of things could happen that don't. Now, forget it,

for God's sake. Bones was a working stiff who fell off a truck. That's all there was to it, so forget anything I said."

I promised that I would, and we went on down to where the chow was.

Everything was steaming hot to prevent spoilage. Sometimes, you got a little ice in your drinking water and the canned milk would usually be mixed with ice water. But there was no ice for food. The only time you got cold food on the pipelines was in the winter when you didn't want it.

All the food was served plain; that is, without gravies or sauces. No pipeliner would have touched anything with sauce or gravy on it, just as none would have eaten hash or chili or anything like that. They had to be able to see what they were eating, to know exactly what it was. Anyone who's ever had a bad case of dysentery will know why.

Four Trey and I filled platters with food and drew bowls of boiling coffee. We carried them over to where a group of guys were eating and sat down alongside them on the fill from the ditch. I'd just taken a big mouthful of baked beans when one of them called to me.

"Hey, Tommy. You seen the chippy yet?"

Chippy?

I choked and coughed, almost strangling. Four Trey gave me a long slow look, but I went on coughing, pretending not to notice. I also pretended like I couldn't answer the guy who'd called to me, and he spoke again, pointing.

"She's camped off over in there, Tommy. I was standing up on the truck coming out this morning and I got a good look at her. *Wowee,* what a babe!"

"I seen her, too," another guy said, and a couple of others

chimed in that they'd also seen her. "Come payday I'm really gonna have some of that!"

I went on eating, forcing the food down, my face on fire with shame and anger. I wanted to stomp every one of them, and I couldn't even object to what they were saying. If I'd had a hold of Carol right then, I'd have shaken her until her teeth rattled.

"I'll tell you what I'm gonna do"—the first guy was speaking again. "I'm gonna pay that little doll a visit tonight. I'll bet if I talk to her right, I can get it on credit until payday. Why...."

"Save yourself a trip," Four Trey said. "She wouldn't trust you for a penny of it."

"Yeah? You talk like you know, man."

"I do. I was over to see her last night."

It was a lie, of course, but they didn't know that. I doubt if there was another person in the world who knew that he was impotent.

"No, sir," Four Trey went on. "That little gal doesn't trust no one for nothing. I had some dough; more than enough, I thought. But it wasn't enough for her, and she wouldn't wait for even a dollar of it."

"Yeah? How much did she want, anyway?"

Four Trey said that she wanted twenty bucks, and he held up his hand at their grunts of surprise and disbelief.

"I know, I know, boys. Three to five bucks is the going price, but it's not going for her. Either you pay twenty or you can stay in your sack and dream about it."

"Maybe not"—from a big loose-lipped guy. "Maybe I get it without payin' nothing."

Four Trey gave him a pitying smile. "You mean you think you can take it away from her?"

"She wouldn't be the first one I took it from!"

"Probably not," Four Trey nodded evenly. "But you'd probably be the first guy to have his bellybutton next to his asshole. The little lady has a sawed-off twelve-gauge and she knows how to use it."

He stood up, lifting his tray and bowl with him. I stood up with him, and he looked down at the guy with a smile that would have chilled a Polar bear.

"Maybe you'd better try it," he said. "Or maybe you'd just better drag-up and get out of camp tonight. Because if I ever see you again, I'm going to swing at you with a rock drill."

"And I'll be swinging right along with you," I said.

The guy looked down at the ground. No one said anything, and finally he moved his head in a little jerk. He'd leave camp. He knew that he'd better.

Four Trey and I walked back up the line to the place where we'd been shooting. He stopped there, and I stopped with him. Wanting to thank him or to explain; to say something or do something—I didn't know just what.

"Well, Tommy." He began drawing on his gloves. "You'd better be getting up to those jackhammers, hadn't you?"

"I'm going right now," I said. "I . . . I got to tell you something, Four Trey. I know what you're thinking, but. . . ."

"What I think, Tommy, is that a kid with a great potential is about to throw it all down the drain. But that's his business, as long as he keeps it his. If it ever again gets to crowding in on mine, as it did this morning. . . ."

"Four Trey," I said, "I wasn't lying when I said I'd been thinking about Bones' death. It *has* bothered me."

"It has, huh?" He gave me a look of cynical amusement. "Been losing a lot of sleep over it, have you? Not that pipeline chippy out there, but poor old anonymous Bones."

"All right," I said doggedly. "I was just trying to explain, but have your own way about it."

"Maybe I'd better explain something to you, Tommy. The mortality rate on pipeline jobs is approximately one death to every ten miles of line. Since we've already had one death, in our burial of Brother Bones—how's that for alliteration, Tommy?—and since we've made a little less than five miles of line, I'd say you need have no fear of the grim reaper for another day or two."

He bent down, began looking for the shot-holes which the jackhammers had drilled.

I turned away and began trudging up-line.

In the scorching midday heat, everything rested but man. Quail and pheasant hid beneath the sage and chaparral, wings hung loosely from their bodies, their undersides wallowed into the dust. Cottontails, whole families of them, napped in the wind-cooled stands of grass. Giant mule-jacks stood like sleepy sentries under the needly groves of Spanish Bayonet. Prairie dogs dreamed in the sparse shade of their mounds.

All the life of this wild and lonely land was there to see . . . for those with the eyes to see it. Nothing took cover. Nothing ran from you. Having seen no men before, they saw no need to hide or run.

I stopped to light a cigarette, and a long, thick shape slid frantically across the blistering earth and began to wind itself around the relative coolness of my leg. It was a bull snake, all of five feet long with a middle as thick as my biceps. I let it rest for a minute, then gently unwound it. It struck at me with its head, its only weapon. But the blows were lazy, heat-drugged; and the snake, finding himself unhurt, ceased them immediately. I put it inside my shirt, let it cool in my evaporating sweat. When I took it out, transferring it to the interior of a joint of pipe, it was blissfully asleep.

There were two jackhammers. Two men, spelling one another, worked each jackhammer. I took the place of a guy who'd had so much of it that even a mormon board looked good to him. He didn't know mormon boards, I guess, or maybe he just had an awful hate for jackhammers. Which is a mighty easy thing to get.

You've probably seen jackhammers—or airhammers, to use their proper name. They're used in breaking up pavement and the like. They have a two-handed grip across the top, in the shape of an elongated oval, with a heavy air-cylinder extending down from it. A steel drill fits into the end of the cylinder, and when the air is cut in that drill begins to vibrate and bounce about umpteen times a second.

It's not the only thing that vibrates, either, as you may have noticed. Hanging onto that jackhammer is like holding onto a steel wildcat with St. Vitus' dance. It shakes you from your shoesoles to your eyeballs, and little chips of rock sting your hide like birdshot, and I guess God must have his ears plugged to the noise because he sure wouldn't put up with it if he could hear it.

On pavement jobs, the jackhammer work is only a few minutes at a time; on the pipeline, it's almost steady. When you run out of rock, you move right ahead until you find some more. And if you don't move real fast, if that jackhammer stops popping and rattling for more than a minute or two, you've got high-pressure on your tail.

Two strawbosses ran a check on us that afternoon; one of Depew's men also came by to check our time and note my change of jobs. Then, a little after four in the afternoon, Higby drove up.

My partner and I had been taking fifteen-minute runs on the hammer. It was my turn to rest, and I was sitting on the ditch fill when Higby arrived. He gave me a sharp look, started to say something I guess; then figured out the situation—that I wasn't just loafing—and came over and sat down by me.

"How's it going, Tommy?"

I shook my head, shrugged.

"How'd you like to run a hammer . . . steady?"

I laughed, still not saying anything. Higby grinned sourly, then made his voice persuasive.

"You run a nice hammer, Tommy. And it's a lot safer than powder. You just check back over your memory and tell me if you ever saw an old powder monkey."

I said I'd never seen any old jackhammer men either. Then I looked at him frowning, struck by the strangeness of his urging a change of jobs on me.

"I work with Four Trey," I said. "That was the understanding when I hired on. I help on powder with him and I deal blackjack for him as soon as. . . ."

"That's still the understanding, as long as you cut the stuff and Four Trey wants you. I had the impression, however, that you didn't care too much about shooting powder."

"I like it all right," I said. "I like it just fine. Now, unless Four Trey's got some complaints. . . ."

"I imagine he'd tell us both if he had." Higby shook his head. "But I'm sure he'd be willing to change helpers if I asked him to. And there'd be no trouble about finding him one. There's always someone willing to shoot powder. Someone with so little imagination that he can't picture himself getting killed or maimed, or who actually *wants* to get killed. You find a lot of those, too, around the big labor camps."

"Four Trey's got plenty of imagination," I said. "He sure as hell doesn't want to get killed, either, and neither do I."

"I'd like to see you stay on jackhammer, Tommy. You could make a lot of overtime."

"Yeah," I said. "And who can take it?"

"It's good for a man. Keeps him out of trouble. A man puts in a long day on a jackhammer, and he doesn't want anything but bed."

I said I'd been keeping out of trouble long before I ever fitted hands to a jackhammer and I figured I still knew the secret. He nodded and stood up, dusting the seat of his pants. I got up, too, since it was about time to go back to work;

kind of wondering about his mention of keeping out of trouble. It might mean that he'd somehow found out about Carol, but I didn't see how he could have. Certainly, Four Trey would never, never have butted into my affairs by asking him to talk to me.

I went back to work, deciding that it was just a generality tossed off during a conversation. He'd stopped for a breather and used the time to make a hard sell on jackhammers. He needed operators badly so he'd pulled out all the stops, getting a lot more personal than a pipeline boss ordinarily would have.

He spoke to the other men briefly, about what I couldn't hear because of the noise of my hammer. Then he started walking up the line route, stopping every now and then to make a little marker of piled-up rock. He made approximately twenty of them in the space of about five hundred yards, then came back to his pickup and drove off toward camp.

Those markers were places where we had work to do. There appeared to be enough of them to keep us busy through noon tomorrow, if not longer. I mentioned this to my partner when it came his turn on the hammer, and he gave me a sore look.

"Lay off, pal. I ain't in the mood for kidding."

"Kidding? What are you talking about?"

"The big boy didn't tell you, huh?" He shook his head grimly. "We do that tonight. Every damned bit of it before we button up the day."

"*Tonight?* But . . . but, dammit to hell . . . !"

"Can't do it, hmmm? Just ain't up to it? Well, don't bother to tell the man, because I already done it and he just didn't believe me at all. He said I must mean that I wanted to drag-up my time, and if I didn't mean that I'd better get hot on this hammer."

"Gee," I said, "I was just going to ask if I couldn't work over."

He grinned tiredly, spat dust from his mouth and scoured his hands against his pants. I turned the hammer over to him, and he gave it a boost with his knee, brought the drill down on a patch of rock and cut in the air.

It began to shake, rattle and roar. He bore down on it, arms stiff, and it whined and clattered and tried to jump away from him. His teeth clenched with the effort to hold on, and his whole body jerked and vibrated.

I moved back away from the noise and dropped down on the fill. I began to massage my legs and arms, groaning when I hit a knotted muscle and wondering what Carol would think when I didn't show up.

I figured that she'd probably be pretty upset about it, that she'd maybe think I was sore and wasn't coming back. I looked up the line at the work that remained to be done and I decided that we might get through in time for me to pay her a quick call. A doggone quick one, just long enough to say hello and let her know I wasn't sore. Because I sure wasn't up to or interested in anything else tonight.

Like Higby had said, all you wanted after a hard day on the hammer was bed. Just a bed, with no one in it to crowd you.

At five o'clock a kitchen flunky in a company pickup brought supper to us. It was packed into five-gallon lard cans: one for coffee, another for beef, chicken and ham, another for bread-and-butter, cookies and doughnuts, and the remaining two for potatoes and mixed vegetables. We ate all we could hold and put a few doughnuts and cookies in our pockets. The flunky dumped everything that was left over onto the prairie, then drove back down the line toward camp.

We had a cigarette or two . . . makin's since none of us had any ready-rolled. The we matched for turns on the hammers, stepped up the speed of the generator and went back to work.

It was almost ten o'clock by the time we had finished, and long jagged streaks of lightning were crackling across the black sky, seeming to rip it apart like a curtain, then to sew it back up with thunder.

I rode in the seat with Higby going into camp, and he kept sticking his head out the window, feeling for rain. He looked as tired as I felt and he seemed to get older with each crack of lightning. A hard rain, one that continued through tomorrow, would stop work on the line. Even a hard night's rain would set the job back, but for only a few hours with any kind of luck. The blazing sun and the constant wind dried things up fast. You could toss a dipper of water on the ground, and it would evaporate almost before it landed.

Higby swore under his breath, sidled a worried glance at me. "Well, Tommy? What do you think?"

"Nothing to it," I shrugged. "Nothing more than a spring shower."

He said he sure as hell hoped I was right, and I lied that I'd bet money on it. I figured that he already knew that only a fool or a stranger prophesies the weather in West Texas, and there was no point in reminding him of it.

97

Camp was dark except for the water-barrel lantern and the lantern in the truck-parking area. Higby brought the pickup to a stop, spoke to me quietly as I started to climb out.

"A hell of a hard day, huh, Tommy? I imagine you can't wait to hit the sack."

"Well . . ." I hesitated. "If there's something you want to talk to me about, Mr. Higby . . ."

"No, no, bed's the best place for you. I guess you know I'll want you on the hammers again tomorrow."

"I figured," I said. "But that wraps it up, right? I'm down for powder monkey's helper and I'll be back to it after tomorrow."

"Stay on the hammers, Tommy," he said softly. "You'll be glad you did later. Stay there and make your overtime and keep out of trouble, and. . . ."

And that was as far as he got. Because I was about as exhausted as a man can get and every nerve of my body was raw, and that second mention of keeping out of trouble— well, it was too damned much. I was in plenty of trouble right then, and I'd got it all from being put on those lousy hammers.

"Look!" I exploded. "What the hell is this, Mr. Higby? What does the top man on a big pipeline job care what happens to a working stiff like me? Why are you bothering with me? What am I to you, anyway? I appreciate your sticking up for me with Depew, but. . . ."

"You don't owe me a thing, Burwell. I did what I had to do; what I thought was right. And you'd better make that *Mr.* Depew."

His voice was stony cold. It yanked me out of my mad like

a skyhook, made me realize that I was way, way out of line in talking up to him.

"I'm sorry, Mr. Higby," I said. "Really sorry. If you want me on a hammer. . . ."

"I don't. You'll go back on powder tomorrow morning."

"But . . . you're not going to fire me, then?"

He shook his head. "I laid myself open for back-talk from a punk. It's my own fault that I mistook him for a man. No"—he cut me off before I could interrupt. "No, I'm not going to fire you, Burwell. Not for this. If I did, I'd probably lose Four Trey along with you. And he has friends who might pull out if he did, and his friends have friends, and . . . So you're safe, Burwell—for now, at least."

"I'm sorry," I said, miserably. "I ought to have my tail kicked."

"You're not worth it." He opened the door on his side and started to get out. "I've wasted too much time on you already."

He gave me a curt nod, strode away toward the high-pressure tent. I got out and went over to the wash bench.

It would be hard to tell you how I felt. Shabby, cheap, crummy—all those things and a lot more besides. A tinhorn through and through. A good man had tried to befriend me, and I'd thrown dirt in his face. It was a low-down thing to do, a punk thing, and I felt as low as a guy could get.

I made a pass at washing up. I went through the walkway between the tents, headed across the prairie toward the place where Carol was camped. Somehow, I wasn't very set-up about seeing her tonight. I was even a little annoyed when I thought of her, which was unfair, but understandable.

Except for her, my touchiness about seeing her, I wouldn't have blown up with Higby. Except for her, I would still have been aces with Four Trey, instead of having him half-leery of me.

I'd considered myself a man, a guy who'd finally grown up and come to grips with himself. I'd been a man, and a little ol' gal barely five feet tall had made me forget that I was.

I didn't know then that the right girl can do that to a man and that it's the surest sign that he is one. I was too miserable, too anxious to push some of my blame on someone else.

I went stumbling across the pitch-dark prairie, brooding, muttering to myself. I caught my toe in a prairie-dog hole and fell down and I remained flopped for a moment, rehearsing a little speech I intended to make.

"Now, I'm telling you, girl. You're going to straighten up and knock off the nuttiness or it's going to be down on the mope-pole for you! I've had just a big plenty, and from now on. . . ."

There was a crash—the damnedest one I ever hope to hear. A great bayonet of lightning speared down past my head, and a plume of white fire leaped up from the ground to meet it. There was a blinding flash, literally blinding. The prairie was suddenly as bright as blazing day. I closed my eyes against it. I opened them again on a world that was suddenly so dark that I thought I had lost my sight.

And then it began to rain. Not drops, but streams, rivers and lakes and oceans of water.

It can be a long time between rains in Far West Texas. A

year, sometimes two years. Nature doesn't get around to the place often, and she has to make up for lost time when she does. And she must have had a lot to make up for tonight.

I couldn't see. I could hardly take a deep breath without drowning. I started running, falling and stumbling at every step. I became completely turned-around, losing all track of where Carol's housecar was or the camp was or I was.

I started traveling in what I hoped was a circle, but I didn't make a very good go of it, I guess, because it was hours before I reached the line. I began following it, following it the wrong way at first and ending up at the far end. I turned around and started back the other way. And then, as abruptly as it had begun, the rain stopped.

Not another drop fell. It simply stopped as suddenly as though a faucet had been closed.

It was dawn by then. When I finally reached camp, the sun was creeping up over the horizon.

It was going to be another scorching hot day. Which meant nothing at all to me at the moment. I was chilled through one side and out the other and I wanted to thaw out at the kitchen range and drink four or five gallons of scalding coffee.

I headed for it by the quickest route—through the entrance to the chow tent and on back to the rear. I had my head down, hurrying, and I almost tripped over the booted leg which swung lazily out in front of me.

"Now, let's just slow down a little, sonny."

"Wha'—!" I jerked my head up, startled. "What's going on?"

Four men were seated at the head of the table, a tin bowl

of coffee in front of each. Higby and Depew sat on the far side, next to the tent wall. The man who had stuck out his boot and another man sat on the aisle where I was.

They might have been in their thirties, forties or even their early fifties. It was hard to say with their type. They had leathery sun-seamed faces, and their foreheads looked burned beneath the brims of their tilted-back Stetsons. They were broad-shouldered but thin-hipped, and their booted feet looked preposterously small. Both wore guns at their hips, weapons which somehow fitted-in and blended with the lanky bodies like congruent parts of them.

The man who had first spoken to me took a small notebook from the pocket of his checked shirt. He wet his thumb, turned a page or two, then nodded and raised his eyes again.

"Burwell. Thomas Burwell. Been out all night, Tom?"

"Yes, I mean, yes, sir," I said.

"Uh-hah," he nodded approvingly, sliding a twinkling-eyed glance at his companion. "Nice young fella, ain't he, Hank? Got his manners about him. Reckon he ought to have some hot coffee and breakfast in him, straight off, don't you?"

"No more than fittin'," drawled the other man. "Know I'd sure want some if I'd been out in the rain all night. I sure would, an' that's a fact, Pete. You want to write it down in that little book of yours, I'll be proud to swear to it."

I looked from one to the other, fear mingling with my weariness. A cold lump formed around my heart, and I shivered. And nervous half-hysterical laughter welled up in my throat. Pete's twinkling eyes narrowed, and he spoke regretfully to Hank.

"Seems to think it's funny, Thomas Burwell does. Reckon maybe he ain't such a nice young fella after all."

"Aw, pshaw, now," Hank protested. "He just ain't got his bearin's yet. Needs his coffee an' vittles t'get himself organized. Reckon we ought t' feed him an' then warn him, an', by ding, I bet he don't do no laughin' at all, then!"

Warn me? The lump around my heart grew larger and colder. I looked at Higby, and he bit his lip and looked away. I looked at Depew, noting his expression of smug contentment. Pete scratched his chin thoughtfully, his eyes fixed on a point just above my head. He sighed, recrossed his boots and nodded to Hank.

"Seems like you got the right of it, pardner. The Man says so, an' the books says so an' besides which it's only decent. Thomas Burwell, you are under arrest on suspicion of murderin' one Albert 'Bud' Lassen, an' anything you say may be used against you and what d'you want for breakfast?"

The dragline was parked about four hundred yards out of camp, a few hundred yards from the start of the line. There was no use for it at this stage of the work, and the lay of the land made it difficult to move it about. So it had been left there, out of the way, until it was needed.

Just before the rain started, the night guard on the pipeline had heard a loud crash—the sound of the dragline bucket dropping. Hurrying over to investigate, he had found Bud's body. The bucket had dropped on him, its two halves open, virtually cutting him in two as it smashed him into the ground. The long, sharp, steel prongs had gone through his body in a dozen places.

The guard had notified Higby. Despite the rain, Higby made it in to town and called the Matacora sheriff's office. Apparently, the downpour wasn't a general one, and the two deputies had gotten most of the way here before they had had to stop. They had come the rest of the way this morning, arriving in camp in their big high-backed Stearns-Knight about an hour before I did.

". . . uh, huh, I see," Pete nodded encouragingly. "You left camp right after you finished work, an' went to see your gal. So naturally you couldn't been over at that whatchmacallit, dragline, killin' old Bud."

"I wouldn't have been killing him, anyway," I said. "But. . . ."

"That little ol' gal said you never come near her last night. You was supposed to, but you didn't."

"All right," I said. "I've been trying to tell you. I was going to see her, but. . . ."

"Oh, you was goin' to, but you didn't. Which means that you must have been somewheres else. Wouldn't you say it seemed that way to you, Hank?"

"Seems as though," Hank drawled. "It plumb does, an' that's a fact."

"You know how to run one of them, uh, draglines, Thomas?"

"No. Well, I know how; I mean, I know the principle of it. But. . . ."

"Ever been arrested, Thomas? Ever been tried and convicted?"

"Well, sure," I said. "I bet everyone in camp has at one time or another. You know, things like drunk and disorderly, and vagrancy and . . . well, things like that."

"Just things like that, hah? Nothin' else?"

"I'll tell you," Hank said. "I'll bet me a nickel, Pete, that this here young fella is an' a. and b. 'er. I'd bet a whole nickel an' I wouldn't ask for no change."

"Thomas, you know what a. and b. is?"

"Assault and battery," I said. "But, dammit, that's just another way of saying self-defense. It was in my case, anyhow. The other guys started it, and I finished it."

"Mmm. What about yesterday morning when you jumped all over ol' Bud? The way I get it, he hadn't bothered you none a-tall."

"Well, all right," I said. "But. . . ."

"Said you was goin' t'kill him, didn't you? Might've done it right then an' there, if you hadn't been dragged off of him."

"That's right, officer," Depew interjected. "And I'm sure he *did* kill Lassen last night. He had the opportunity and the motive, and. . . ."

"You told me. Now, Thomas. . . ."

"Officer, I don't understand your attitude. Why do you continue to shilly-shally and delay when. . . ."

"You already told him," Hank said. "He already told you, didn't he, Pete?"

"Maybe I didn't understand him real good," Pete said. "Mr. Depew, are you sayin' that you're absolutely positive, beyond the shadow of a doubt, that Thomas killed Bud Lassen?"

"Yes, I am positive! Anyone with half a brain would be!"

"Well, now," Pete said. "That's different. Now, we're gettin' somewhere. You got a car, Mr. Depew?"

"Car? Why, yes. It's back home with my wife, but. . . ."

"What's the license number?" Pete waited. "What's your wife's birthday?" He waited again. "What's the date of your wedding anniversary?" Another wait. "You mean, you don't know, Mr. Depew? You mean a plumb positive fella like you, that's absolutely positive about things that ain't a God-dang bit of his business, don't even know the license number of his car or when his wife was born or the date he first started diddlin' her? Well, now, that's plumb surprisin', ain't it, Hank?"

"Amazin'." Hank stared hard at Depew. "Fella like that probably wouldn't know which end of his dingus to pee with. Ain't that right, Mr. Depew? *I said, ain't that right, Mr. Depew?*"

Depew looked from one to the other, his face blazing. He stumbled to his feet suddenly and almost ran out of the tent. Higby spoke for the first time.

"Gentlemen, we're going to have to give the men their breakfast here pretty pronto. If you'd like to move to one of the other tents. . . ."

Pete drawled that that wouldn't be necessary. "Got all we need for the present, wouldn't you say so, Hank? Got all we need here, right now?"

"A plumb plenty," Hank agreed. "An' that's a fact."

"Thomas, you want anything more besides that coffee? Got anything you want to take with you?"

"W-With . . . ? Take with me where?"

He told me where. To Matacora, the county jail. "Got anything, you better take it along. Might be gone quite a spell."

"You sure might, Thomas." Hank wagged his head solemnly. "Yes, sir, you sure as heck might. I'd bet a nickel on it, even money, an' I wouldn't ask for no change."

The county seat of Matacora was actually two towns, rather than one. There was the very old one, built around the courthouse square, with its roots in the ranching industry; a town of substantial brick and sandstone buildings, with sheet-metal awnings extending out over the sidewalks. Surrounding and abutting this was the new town, the one that had sprung up with the discovery of oil: The usual boomtown collection of machine shops, honky-tonks, flop houses, and what-have-you, plus—since the oil money was relatively old here—a considerable number of structures which would have looked good even in a large city.

My cell was in the top of the courthouse tower, a kind of cupola perched high above the steep slate roof. There were windows on all four sides, and I could see every section of town and for miles beyond. The distant ranch houses, and the oil derricks, and the cars and trucks creeping along the roads—it was all spread out there below me. There were trains, too, both freight and passenger, the first trains I'd seen in a long time. I watched a couple of them making up in the yards, then huffing and puffing out of town, slowly gathering speed as they rolled out onto the prairie and at last fading away into the brilliant sunlight. I watched those trains and when I sat back down on my bunk my eyes were watering so bad I was almost blind.

I got them cleared finally and rolled myself a cigarette. I started thinking again, my mind moving around in circles as it tried to latch onto something hopeful.

Bud Lassen had been pretty generally detested around the Matacora sheriff's office. Without actually saying so, the two deputies who'd arrested me had made that clear. Nonetheless, Bud had been one of them; he'd been on their side, a cop. And a guy who beat up a cop was automatically their enemy.

You just didn't beat up cops. You just didn't threaten to kill them. To their way of thinking, either of those things was reason enough for Bud to have killed me, and the only mistake he'd made was in not doing it. To their way of thinking, I'd proved myself guilty, and they saw no reason to try to disprove it.

I'd been jailed a little before noon and I saw no one the rest of that day except the elderly turnkey who brought me my meals. Early the next morning, right after breakfast, he herded me out of the cell and down to the sheriff's office, where I was turned over to a deputy I hadn't seen before. The latter gestured lazily, waving me toward the door of a small anteroom. I went into it, and there was Four Trey Whitey.

"How's it going, bo?" He winked at me, holding out his hand. "Looks like you're holding your own with 'em."

"Four Trey. . . . Oh, gosh, Four Trey!" I said, and then I bit my lip, getting ahold of myself. "How's it with you?"

"I'll make it as soon as I stop rattling inside. I've been riding a supply truck since three this morning. I've got to be starting back in about an hour, so. . . ."

He jerked his head, signalling me to come in close. I did so, and he lowered his voice.

"You're getting out of here, Tommy. They're going to let you go."

"Huh?" My heart skipped a beat "Holy gosh . . . !"

"Keep your voice down! They don't know it yet. And you're not supposed to know it, so don't let on. You'll blow it if you do."

"But . . . but. . . ." I gestured helplessly. "Why . . . I mean, how. . . ."

"Never mind how or why. I don't have time to explain. Just take my word for it that it's going to happen. All you have to do is keep your mouth shut and wait."

"I'll sure do that," I said. "How long will it be, Four Trey?"

"Not long. Are you sweating for anything? How's the chow?"

I told him that the chow was good, but I could use some cigarettes and maybe something to read. "I'd ask for pencil and paper, if I was going to be here any length of time. But. . . ."

"I'll see that you get everything you need," he said. "Cigarettes, reading material, everything. Now, I've got something else to tell you. A couple of things." He took a long pull on his cigarette, blew smoke from his nostrils. "Do you remember that big bust we went on in Dallas? When you wound up with the d.t.'s?"

"I'm not likely to forget it," I said. "I blew damned near six thousand dollars on it."

"No, you didn't, Tommy. You blew around fifteen hundred."

"The heck I did. I had almost six grand to begin with, and. . . ."

"I took forty-five hundred of it. I knew it would get away from you if I didn't, so I took it. It's deposited right here in your name in the First State Bank of Matacora."

I stared at him wordlessly, my mouth wide open in surprise. Four Trey nodded evenly.

"I was going to tell you after this job was finished. I figured you'd have enough sense by that time, if you were ever going to have enough, to know how to use it. But in view of what's happened. . . ."

"My gosh," I said. "I . . . I just can't believe it, Four Trey. Me with a whole forty-five hundred dollars, and . . . and . . . I hardly know what to say."

Four Trey said not to say anything; just to get the hell away from the kind of life I was leading and go to college like I'd always talked about doing.

"I'm going to count on your doing that, Tommy. For your sake, I hope I'm not mistaken."

"Well," I said, kind of looking away from him. "It's certainly a lot of money. I sure can't claim that I don't have the money for college."

"And?"

"And I'm sure obliged to you," I said, still not looking at him. "Here I thought I was flat broke, and all the time I. . . ."

"Don't do it, Tommy. I'm warning you, don't do it."

"Uh, do what?" I said.

"You have no job on the line. I'm through with you, and so is Higby. There's nothing for you out here any more. And when I say nothing I'm including that little whore you've been seeing."

"She's not a whore! I don't care how it looks—what any-one says—she's not a. . . ."

"She isn't, huh?" He chuckled grimly. "Then I wonder why almost a dozen welders visited her after chow last night. I wonder why they claimed she was the best they ever had."

I gulped, feeling like I'd received a hard kick in the stomach. Feeling all the blood drain out of my face.

Welders. They were all well-heeled, carrying heavy. They wouldn't have needed to wait until payday.

"Tommy. . . ." There was a pitying note in Four Trey's voice. "I'm sorry, Tommy. I wish I hadn't had to tell you that."

"That's all right," I said. "What the hell, anyway?"

"That's it. What the hell? It's hard for you to believe now, but this is the best thing that could have happened to you. You'll meet some nice girl later on, and. . . ."

"Do you mind?" I said. "Do you mind if we just don't talk about it? For God's sake, why do you have to keep talking about it? I mean if that's the way it is, why . . . why. . . ."

"Sure," Four Trey said softly, "whatever you say, kid."

We didn't talk much after that. I promised to write him after I was settled, and he promised to write me. He said maybe he'd come to see me after the job was buttoned up, and I said I'd count on it. Then, the deputy opened the door and said that time was up. So Four Trey and I shook hands, and I went back to my cell.

For a time, I felt about as lousy as a man can feel. Even the fact that I was getting out of jail didn't cheer me up. After what Four Trey had told me about Carol, I didn't think I could ever feel good again. I had the blues so bad that I didn't even glance at the package of magazines and stuff that the turnkey tossed through the bars. And then, right when I was at my glummest, I suddenly laughed out loud. I laughed and I got mad, so sore that if Four Trey had been there right then I think I would have socked him.

Because he'd lied about Carol. All I had to do was think about it a while, and I knew he had lied.

Those welders wouldn't be lining up for any pipeline whore. Most of them had wives and families, and they'd just come from those wives and families. They'd have to be a hell of a lot harder up than they were now before they went for a woman, and when they did it wouldn't be the kind you'd find out here. They had too much at stake, too much to lose by fouling themselves up.

Well, sure, there might be one nut in the group. There's always someone who just doesn't know when he's well off. But a dozen? Never! Four Trey had laid it on a little too thick.

I bunked in early after supper, the light being too poor for reading or writing. For that matter, my mind was too full of plans for Carol and me and that forty-five hundred dollars to think about anything else. So I just lay there in the semi-darkness, listening to the distant sounds from the street, smoking and day-dreaming—if a guy can day-dream at night—and putting all sorts of schemes together.

Four Trey hadn't said just when they were setting me free. But I figured that it would just about have to be by tomorrow night, or, at the very latest, by breakfast the next morning. I would have been in custody seventy-two hours by then, which was as long as I could be held on suspicion. They'd have to either charge me with murder or release me. And since they apparently didn't have a case or they had a more likely suspect. . . .

Well, anyway, I was getting out. Four Trey wouldn't have kidded me about that. He couldn't tell me exactly when, probably because he knew how the law would feel about a character who backtalked and roughed-up a cop. He knew they'd give me a hard time as long as they could get away with it. But I *was* getting out.

I fell asleep at last, dreaming about Carol and going to college and God knows what-all. Smiling when I thought of how surprised she'd be when I showed her the forty-five hundred and told her to start moving because we were going to get long-gone from pipeline camps, and we were going to stay gone.

I had a hell of a good sleep that night. Most of the night, that is. The one time I didn't came around three in the morning, when Four Trey's sardonic face suddenly loomed up before me; a bitter, contemptuous face with eyes as cold as ice. I squirmed under their stare, silently mumbling a question:

Why was he looking at me like that? And his reply came to me as clearly as if he had been real, right there in the cell with me, instead of a dream.

"I know she's not a whore. Now, give me the rest of it."

"The rest?"

"You heard me, you lousy punk! The real reason you're coming back!"

I said, "What the hell are you talking about?" Then, I said, "Ouch!" because I had sat up abruptly, bumping my head on the bunk above me.

I rubbed my skull drowsily, wondering what had awakened me, the dream gone from my mind for the moment. Then, I snuggled back under the covers and went to sleep and I was still sleeping when the turnkey called me for breakfast.

About an hour after breakfast, he took me to a shower room, and I had a bath and a shave while he looked on.

After that I was taken before a judge and charged with first-degree murder.

Like most public officials in that area, the county attorney held his job as a sideline. He was a rich man, rich from cattle and oil, and most of his time was spent taking care of his wealth. His being county attorney was just a gesture at public service or civic responsibility or some such thing—whatever a man calls it when he takes the credit for something that others do for him. His next step up probably would be some kind of state office, then maybe the governor's chair or congress. Right now, the duties of his office were being carried out by a couple of young deputies, and he was pretty irritated with me for insisting on seeing him.

"What the hell's eating on you, Burwell? The boys made a clear-cut case against you, so naturally you were booked. There's nothing I can do about it."

"But the case isn't clear-cut! It could easily have been an accident. . . ."

"We don't think so. Frankly, I'd have killed the son-of-a-bitch myself if he'd hung around this town much longer. Caught him kicking a horse one time. But the way you went about it . . . well, that's bad. If you'd killed him in a fair fight, I'd have stood in line to shake your hand, but. . . ."

"I didn't kill him! We'd made up our differences!"

"Mmm?" He glanced at a paper on his desk. "We've got a witness who swears you didn't make up with him. Fella named Wingy Warfield. He claims Lassen offered to shake hands with you and you refused."

"But Wingy's a loudmouth! He'll say anything to hear himself talk! What actually happened was . . . was. . . ."

"Yes?" He squinted at me thoughtfully, seemingly caught by something in my manner. "What's the matter with you, Burwell?"

"Matter?" I said. "What do you mean?"

"We've got a big-plenty of reason to hold you. Even I know that much, and I don't know a Goddamned thing about evidence. But you act like you were absolutely sure of being freed." He waited, continuing to squint at me. "Someone promise you something, boy? You just tell me who it was, and I'll skin the ass right off of 'em!"

Well, of course, I had been sure of getting out, but I couldn't say so in view of Four Trey's warning. So I mumbled around a little bit, saying that naturally I didn't think they could hold an innocent man, and I *was* innocent, by gosh! And he stopped staring at me and began to fidget again.

"For God's sake, boy!" He suddenly cut in on me. "That's the way it is, so that's the way it is! Got yourself a lawyer yet?"

"I think so," I said. "I think there was a lawyer when I went before the judge this morning, but. . . ."

"Oh, that shitass! I mean a *real* lawyer." He glanced at his watch, then rose abruptly, rocking in his boots. "Well, no hurry about it, I guess. You don't come to trial for almost seven weeks yet."

He rammed a ranch-style hat down on his head and started around the desk. I stood up, too, and he dropped an arm around my shoulders and walked me to the door with him.

"Now, tell me, son," he said, pausing on the threshold and turning me around to face him. "Did you kill that son-of-a-bitch or not?"

"No, sir," I said. "I certainly did not kill him."

"Real sure about that, now? You're not lyin' to me?"

"I'm sure," I said. "I'm not lying."

His eyes bored into mine, seeming to look right through me and out the other side. At last he sighed and scowled, rubbing his face with a knotty-looking hand.

"Too Goddamned bad," he grumbled. "If you were guilty,

you could plead to second-degree or manslaughter; I'd certainly agree to it. Did I tell you I saw him kick a horse one time?"

"Yes, sir," I said. "I believe you mentioned something about it."

"But, of course, if you're actually innocent. . . ." He shook his head, scowling, then brightened a little. "Well, you just get yourself a good lawyer. I'll help you if need be. A good man ought to be able to beat the pants off of these boys of mine."

I said I sure hoped he was right. Then, despite the jam I was in, I laughed out loud. I just couldn't help myself.

He gave me a startled look, kind of offended, you know. Then he laughed, too, giving me such a hard clap on the back that I was almost knocked from my feet.

"That's what I like to hear!" he boomed. "Show me something that a good laugh or a stiff drink won't cure, and I'll put in with you. What the hell, anyway? What's the use crying when you can laugh?"

"Yes, sir," I said. "What's the use?"

"You've got money in the bank, right? A nice little stake? So, all right, then. Even if you're convicted you've got no problem. Just flash a little of the long green in front of the Parkers, and they'll have you home ahead of the jury!"

I said, yes, sir, again, and he gave me another clap on the back and told me to keep my dauber up. Then, he hurried off somewhere, on his own private business, I suppose, and I went back to my cell.

Years later, I told a prospective publisher about that county attorney and some of the other people I'd bumped into in the Texas of those days. And long before I'd finished talking, he was shaking his head. People didn't act like that, he flatly assured me. There were no such people. That's what the man said, and I didn't try to talk him out of his ignorance. But he couldn't have been wronger.

There were such people; a big plenty of 'em. Quite a few of them made the history books, and at least two of them, Bud and Sis Parker, became governors of the state.

They were brother and sister, Bud and Sis. Ignorant and lowdown crooked, they had a homespun quality and a folksy gift of gab which got the vote every time. Bud was governor first. When he got impeached, Sis Parker ran for his job, and she went into office on a landslide.

The two of them ran the statehouse together. The joke was that they worked shifts, one of them selling pardons while the other was off-duty. It wasn't quite that bad, of course, but no one did time in Texas if he had a few thousand dollars for the Parkers. Some criminals supposedly bought pardons before they pulled a job, charging it off as business expense. Well. . . .

That was the way things were in those days. And the prospect of buying a pardon after being convicted didn't cheer me up any. At the very best, I'd be in jail for weeks to come and when I thought of what would be happening to Carol during those weeks . . . ! I couldn't eat lunch or supper, just sipping a little coffee and almost gagging on it. I smoked three packages of cigarettes, lighting one as fast as I finished another. Fretting and worrying and wondering what the hell had gone wrong.

Four Trey had been so sure that they were going to free me. Yet how could he have been? What could he have known that they didn't know here? Why couldn't he have told them right then and gotten me out immediately?

The more I thought about it, the more confused I became. My head began to ache like it was going to split, and I knew I was going to be in a bad way if I didn't put my mind on something else. But knowing it was a lot easier than doing it. It was no good trying to read; I'd go through a dozen pages without having the slightest idea of what they were about.

I began to pace the floor, back and forth; back wall to door, side wall to bunk. I stopped, finally, my legs weak from all the turning and twisting; stood leaning against the wall with my eyes closed and the wind pouring over my face like water.

It felt good, the wind. It was something I knew, a familiar friendly thing; the steady Texas wind, which had gone with me wherever I had gone. And it brought back memories of all those places: McCamey, and rigging high-line towers, my pants so stiff from alkali water that they could stand by themselves; a casing-crew out of the town of Chalk, and seeing a guy's head pinched off when a line buckled and looped; a derrick-dismantling job in the field west of Big Springs, swinging from the top of a one hundred and twenty–foot rig and knocking out the cross-bracing until it jigged like a drunken dancer. A honky-tonk in Four Sands, and a man who sat at the same table every day. A man with snowy white hair and an obscenely youthful face—a face like a dirty picture.

He spoke to no one. He hardly moved, except to raise his cheese glass of white-corn whiskey or his jelly glass of choc-beer chaser. He simply sat there staring down at the floor—

and listening. To the wind, it seemed like. Listening to the wind and never quite hearing what he was listening for . . .

I sat back down in my bunk. I picked up paper and pencil and began to write. By the time I had finished, my headache was gone and I was able to sleep. Which was all that I really wanted. What I wrote wasn't important, from any angle, and I balled it up and threw it on the floor. But it went something like this:

*A while ago as I sat here, counting the
cracks in the floor,
Trying to blot out the future, to forget
all that happened before,
I heard a baby crying, and I saw a face
I'd known.
But the kid was dead and the face and
head were crying there alone.
Wailing in infinite sorrow, sucking its
finger tips
Till nothing was left but the marrow
and the feebly gnawing lips.
(But maybe it's the wind, kid./
(Maybe it's the wind.)*

*The devil and a bearded saint peeked
through the door at me.
The devil had a smoky taint, the saint
a golden key.
The devil laughed, and he said to him,
"I keep all whom I take."*

And he bound me there to that very
chair with a ten-foot rattlesnake.
(But maybe it's the wind, kid./
(Maybe it's the wind.)

Yeah, maybe it's the wind, kid, that
aching hungry breeze/ That blows all hell
loose through the lid of one contagious
sneeze/ Or it could be the woman's scream
when the club came down on her back/ Or
the starving hounds on the grassy mounds
where the dead fight off their attack/
Or the gasps for breath as the rope
brings death while mob-fire turns bodies
black/ Or the mad men, the bad men, the sad
and the glad men who bring rape and murder
and sack/ Where the bombs explode and the
shells erode where sinned-against have sinned./
(But maybe it's the wind, kid./
(Maybe it's the wind.)

It was mid-morning when I awakened. I lay with my eyes
half-closed for a time, letting the sunlight seep gradually under
the lids, putting the day off as long as possible. At last I
yawned, stretched and looked around, then suddenly sat up
with a start.

121

The cell door stood open. A man in boots and a blue serge suit was leaning against the wall, reading the poem I'd written the night before. He went on reading, giving me a half-nod without looking up. When he had finally finished (and he took his time about it), he shook his head wryly and tossed the paper back to the floor.

He shouldn't have done that. No one should ever treat a writer's work disrespectfully. If he does it, all right. But never do it yourself. He'll like you a lot better if you spit in his face.

"How are you, Burwell?" he said. "Darrow's the name, Ben Darrow. I'm the sheriff here."

"I'm all right," I said, "and I know who you are. I've heard quite a bit about you, sheriff."

I turned around to the sink and began to wash up. He grinned at me in the mirror, blue eyes glinting in his tanned face. A good-humored, intelligent-looking man in his thirties whom I might have liked under different circumstances. I stared back at him coldly, and he chuckled and winked at me.

"Good news, Burwell. You've been cleared."

"Wha . . . !" I whirled around, my heart doing a big flip-flop. "You . . . you really mean that? You're not just kidding me?"

"Now, of course, I'm not. The boys had the evidence to let you go last night, but I was out of town and they decided to play it cute. God knows why . . ." he shook his head, frowning, "since they certainly didn't have any love for Lassen. But I can promise they'll never do it again."

"But I have been cleared?" I insisted. "There's no doubt about that?"

122

"Absolutely none. Three witnesses swear that Lassen was fooling around the dragline when the bucket dropped on him. He must have triggered something, I suppose, or. . . ."

"Why the hell didn't they say something sooner?"

"Why don't a lot of people? Because they're afraid of getting involved or they were doing something that they shouldn't have. These three birds, for example, had stolen some Jamaica ginger out of the cook tent and were tying on a drunk."

That sounded reasonable, but it left some pretty big questions in my mind. Like how had Four Trey known about the three men and why had he wanted me to keep quiet about them. But this was hardly the time or the place to raise those questions.

"Well, Burwell . . ." he gestured toward the door. "You've missed breakfast. Come on and I'll buy you some."

"Thanks," I said. "But I'll buy my own."

I put on my hat and picked up my bindle. Darrow frowned, laughed uncertainly. "Oh, come on, now! Why so huffy? I'm sorry you were held longer than you should have been. But. . . ."

"I get my own jobs," I said. "I spend my own money. Now, good-bye and give my regards to that zillionaire daddy-in-law of yours."

I went on through the door and started down the steps. Abruptly, I turned around and went back to him.

"I'm sorry," I said. "You did something that made me sore, but I'm sure it wasn't deliberate. Anyway, I had no right to say what I did."

He nodded evenly, his voice little more than a cold whisper.

"You had no right. And I usually answer talk like that in a different way. But no one gets swung on in this jail unless he swings first, and I'm not about to break my own rules. So let me just set you straight on something. . . ."

"Don't," I said. "You don't need. . . ."

But he did need to. I'd hit him in the touchiest spot a man has, and he'd been hit there plenty of times before. And he just couldn't let it go.

"I'm a graduate lawyer, Burwell. I'm also a police academy graduate. This is one of the richest counties in the state, and they can afford the very best sheriff in the state. And that's how I got my job. Because I was the best, and they were willing to pay for it. I was sheriff *before* I was married, Burwell. Before, get me? And the first time my father-in-law offers me a nickel will be the last time!"

He broke off, breathing heavily. I repeated that I was sorry, and he gestured curtly toward the steps. I started down them, and after a moment I heard him following me. We went down them together, neither of us saying anything until we were on the walk outside the courthouse. Then he tapped me on the arm and pointed to a restaurant across the street.

"That look all right to you, Burwell?" he said quietly. "I eat there a lot."

"Whatever you say," I said. "You're buying." And I guess it was the right thing to say, because the grin came back to his face as we started across the street.

I had a big breakfast: bacon and eggs and hot cakes. He settled for coffee, taking a thoughtful sip of it as we faced each other across the table.

"You said I'd made you angry, Burwell. Mind telling me how?"

I told him, admitting that I'd been foolish to take offense. He agreed that I had been, particularly after my temper had landed me in jail as a murder suspect.

"On the other hand," he went on, "I'm kind of glad, in a way, that you did blow up. Anyone that wasn't absolutely on the level wouldn't have done it. Criminals can't afford to be touchy; not in front of cops, at least. They're too much on the defensive to be offensive."

"Well. . . ." I hesitated, buttering a fork-load of hot cake. "If that's a compliment, I don't know how to take it."

He shrugged, dismissing the matter. "I understand that you've come into quite a little money. Over four thousand dollars, right?"

"That's right."

"Then, you won't be going back to the pipeline. You wouldn't in any case, I understand, since they don't want you any longer."

"I've been cleared," I said shortly. "I'm a good all-around man and I'm entitled to a job."

"You've got a bad record, Burwell. Twenty-one years old and you've got a record as long as my arm. Yes," he held up his hand. "I know the good side of it, too. About your schooling and all. But the best man in the world can go wrong in a bad environment, and the pipeline is a bad one. It's been a long time since you've been in anything but bad ones. Now, why not give yourself a break?"

I said I appreciated his advice and I'd give it a lot of thought. He shook his head irritably.

"I don't get you, Burwell. Is it the girl? Is she the reason you're bound and determined to throw your life away?"

"I'm not throwing it away," I said and I pushed back my plate. "That was a fine breakfast, sheriff. I'm obliged to you."

Outside the restaurant, I started to say good-bye, but he didn't give up that easily. He sort of guided me down the street, making talk as we walked along, directing my attention toward the bank where my money was and pausing before the windows of a couple of men's stores, more or less forcing me to look at the array of clothes inside. *City* clothes. Then he moved me on until we were within view of the railroad station.

"There it is, Burwell—Tom," he said. "There's a train east at four o'clock. I want you to be on it."

I asked if he was floating me out of the county. He hesitated, then shook his head like a man who found it hard to do.

"I wish it could be, but I've never believed in enforcing the law by breaking it. So, no, it's not an order. But it's the best damned advice you ever had in your life, Tom. The very damned best!"

"And I'm going to take it," I said. "But there's something I've got to do first."

"You mean ask the girl to go with you?" He sighed, gave me an exasperated look. "Now, you know better than that. If she was looking for a decent life, she wouldn't be where she is."

"I know better," I said. "Anyway, I have to ask her."

He stared at me wearily, started to say something, then shrugged and glanced at his watch. "Well," he said. "I did my best. But I guess there's no way of keeping a rat out of a hole."

He turned and started back up the street. I called after him that he'd see; I'd be just fine and he could count on it. He answered me without looking around, not with words but a laugh.

The ugliest, most dismal laugh I'd ever heard.

The stagecoach left Matacora a little after two in the afternoon, and we were almost four hours traveling the eighty-five miles. The driver let me out in front of the Greek's, then swung the big Hudson around in the dusky darkness and headed south toward Fort Stockton.

I'd got myself dolled up in Matacora; new khakis and under-clothes and everything the barber had to sell. But that made no difference to the Greek. He met me at the door, demanding money before he'd let me sit down; then watched me while I ate to make sure I didn't steal anything.

The food tasted lousy. How could it taste any other way? I thought back on my talk with Darrow. And for a moment I almost wished I'd taken his advice, because I'd suddenly had enough of myself as I was. I'd had it with Tommy Burwell—hobo, junglebird, working stiff, gambler, drunk and what-have-you. I couldn't stand him any more, and the only way of getting away from him was to get him to hell away from here!

All the clothes and barbers in the world wouldn't change anything as long as I lived as I did. Nothing would help but a completely new life.

The Greek tossed my change back at me, without a word of thanks. Just threw it at me, so that I had to do some wild grabbing to keep it from going on the floor. Any other time I might have cussed him out or jumped him. But tonight I merely smiled at him and dropped a penny tip on the counter.

It struck me in the back as I went out the door, but I kept right on going. The way I was determined to stay out of trouble, he could have kicked me in the pants and I'd probably have kissed his foot.

Although they were some five miles away, I could see the lights of camp as I started out of town. I headed toward them, following the truck ruts, my heavy shoes trampling the wiry grass with the sound of secret whispering.

A stingy moon climbed up out of a distant stand of black-jack, and rose slowly into the sky like a sagged-in-the-middle candle. The night wind bustled across the prairie, and the first small stars flickered and winked as though about to blow out. Brave with darkness, a coyote howled eerily. A chorus of dog-wolves began to bark, sounding for all the world like they were scolding someone.

Four Trey had solemnly assured me one time that that was exactly what they *were* doing. They were scolding the moon because their butts were built so close to the ground. I went along with the gag and asked him why the moon; the moon couldn't do anything about it. And he said, exactly—that was the whole point.

He fell asleep about then, the bottle being empty, and there was nothing more said on the subject. Thinking back on it years later, it dawned on me that there'd been nothing more to say. He'd said it all, and what he'd said was pretty profound.

I stopped walking to take a breather, coughing and spitting the dust from my mouth. The spittle had hardly hit the ground before it was swarming with black beetles—tumble-bugs—which rolled it into balls, dust and all, and rolled the balls away to their almost invisible nest-holes in the grass.

Tumble-bugs are scavengers of the prairies, keeping them clean by balling-up and disposing of anything in the way of waste matter. You find a lot of them where there are cattle and horses. In this particular area, I figured they probably didn't have things too good, what with nothing but men and machines around. Industrialization was playing hell with their business—a situation I'd written a nutty piece of doggerel about when I should have been using my time for something better:

> *A tumble-bug, all ragged and black,*
> *Stumbled along with some dung on his back.*
> *He'd worked all the day and half the night,*
> *Making his ball compact and tight,*
> *For with automobiles it was getting harder*
> *To fill the needs of the family larder.*
> *Now, the path on which he plied his trade,*
> *Some campers there a john had made.*
> *Poor bug, now blind with perspiration,*
> *Stumbled into the excavation.*
> *He blew his nose and cleared his eyes,*

129

And looked around in glad surprise.
"Surely," said he, "I am dreaming.
"All around, abundance steaming!
"In my most modest estimation,
"Here's food enough to feed a nation!"
He . . .

Well, I'll leave it at that. It gets kind of dirty from then on.

I went on walking until I was within a couple hundred yards of camp. Veering off to the right there, I aimed myself toward the slight dip in the land where Carol's housecar was parked. It took me about twenty minutes to get to it, her campsite that is. I stopped on the rim above it, looking down into the little hollow, almost calling out to her before I saw that she wasn't there. It was the right place; I couldn't be mistaken about that. But the housecar was gone.

For a moment, I didn't know what to think. Hell, I couldn't think at all, the way I felt. Then, it came to me that she might have moved to higher ground on account of that heavy rain. And, breathing easy again, I started looking for her.

The night wasn't bright enough to see far or well. If you didn't have a pretty good idea of where something might be, you could come within a hundred yards of it and miss it. Carol, of course, had to be parked within a fairly limited area. So I marked it out in my mind and began to search it; moving ahead for fifty yards or so, turning off at a sharp angle for a few hundred yards, moving ahead again and then angling back for another few hundred yards. Crossing and crisscrossing.

I'd done a lot of walking without moving very far from

her original campsite when I heard a car. Despite the fact that even small sounds carry far on the prairie, I almost didn't hear it. It was moving so quietly, the softly powerful purring of its motor blending and all but losing itself in the soughing of the wind.

I'd never heard a car run like that one. Its lights were off. In virtual silence, it rolled across the uneven land, swaying but never jolting, smoothly smoothing out the hillocks and hummocks, a dark shadow blowing through the night. Then, it slid down into that little dip in the land and disappeared.

There was absolute silence for a moment, a moment in which I wasn't sure that I hadn't been dreaming. It ended abruptly with the sound of doors opening—and voices. Carol's and others. Men's voices.

There were three of them. Three men. And they didn't linger with her. I was running forward, thinking, you know, that Carol might need help—although she hadn't sounded like it—when the three suddenly came up out of the hollow. Moving fast and walking swiftly away in the darkness. Ducked behind a bush, I tried to get a good look at them. But I didn't have much luck at it.

They were about middling weight and height. They had beards. They were roughly dressed.

In other words, they might be any three of half the men on the line. And, of course, they were working on the line. They'd headed toward camp—where else would they go out here—and if they were in camp they had to be working.

I stayed hidden behind the bush for several minutes, making sure that they weren't coming back.

Then, I went down to where the car was.

It was Carol's housecar all right. I got inside and started it. It sounded like hell. I turned off the motor and got out of the car. Carol ran up and angrily snatched the keys from my hand.

"Well, smarty?" she said. "What do you have to say for yourself now?"

I didn't know what to say. The car had run like any old car might have, choking and missing as bad as any I'd ever heard.

"Well, it didn't run that way a while ago," I said, but I was no longer so sure of myself. "I know it didn't, and no one can tell me it did!"

"Oh, you!" She stamped her foot. "If you knew anything, you wouldn't have come back here! You didn't have to, dog-gone it! That friend of yours, Mr. Whiteside, he told me he'd turned a lot of money over to you, money he'd been saving for you. And you could have. . . ."

"Four Trey? How come you were seeing Four Trey?" I said.

"Now don't you try to make something out of that, Tommy Burwell! He, well, he knew about us and he was afraid I'd be worried, so naturally. . . ."

"What about those three guys tonight? Were they afraid you'd be worried about me, too?"

She looked at me, lips together tightly. "I don't have to

answer your questions, Mr. Burwell! Just who do you think you are, anyway?"

"Don't you bet any money that you don't have to answer," I said, "because I'm the guy you're just as good as married to and the guy you're *going* to be married to. So just don't you give me any argument!"

Her eyes shifted; lowered. She kicked at a pebble. "You . . . you haven't kissed me, Tommy. I haven't seen you for a long long time, and you haven't even kissed me."

"What about those three guys?"

"Will you kiss me if I tell you?"

"Well, uh, yeah, sure I will," I said. "I mean. . . ."

"And hug me real nice? Mmm?" She edged closer to me, her voice a teasing little-girl whisper. "An' . . . an' . . . after you've hugged an' kissed me real good, will you . . . ?" Her arms went around me, pulling my head down to hers so that she could whisper the last words into my ear. "Will you, Tommy? Just for a little while?"

Well. . . .

It wasn't any little while. More than an hour passed before we came back out of the housecar. Plenty of time for her to think up a good explanation for the three men, if she had needed time to think of one. It was so plausible that I doubted that she did.

She'd had to drive into town for supplies and water. The three men had been loafing around the general store. One of them had a couple of bucks, it seemed, and the others had come along to help him blow it. Which added up to a long walk for practically nothing, but at least broke the monotony of camp. Anyway, they'd helped Carol load her supplies and fill her water barrel. So she could hardly refuse when they asked for a ride back to camp.

"It was safe enough, don't you think so, Tommy? I mean, the storekeeper saw us leaving together. He knew who they were, and if anything happened to me. . . ."

"Why were you driving with your lights off?"

"They just went out. One of the men thought I'd probably jolted a wire loose." She put her arms around me, murmured meekly against my chest. "That's the truth, Tommy. You just try them, and see if they come on."

I didn't see any point to that. Not after my experience in testing the car's motor.

"Tommy," she said, "you shouldn't have come back here. You just shouldn't have, darling. I thought my heart would break when I thought you weren't coming back. But . . . but. . . ." Her voice was suddenly firm. "Leave, Tommy. Right tonight. Don't go over to camp. Just go right back to town and keep going."

"Is that what you want me to do?"

"It's what you should do, honey. What you have to do. Mr. Whiteside made me see that. The longer you delay, the harder it will become. You've been in a lot of trouble already, and if you get in any more—"

"All right," I said. "All right, I'll leave."

"You—you will?"

"I will. But you've got to leave with me."

"B-But—but I can't, darling. Not right away. I'll tell you what"—she gave me a brave bright smile. "You go ahead first. Get a place for us, and get started in school and—and everything—and then I'll join you. How will that be, hmm? Okay, honey?"

I said, no, it sure as heck wasn't okay. She'd either go with me tonight or neither one of us would go.

"I'll tell you something, girlie," I said. "You may have a big lineup of guys over here on payday, but I'm goin' to be right at the head of it. And the first bo that tries to climb into that truck with you is goin' to get fanned with a forgy stick!"

I was about as steamed up as a man can get, and if she'd said one word back to me I'd have done a little fanning right then and there. On the seat of her pants, that is, and it wouldn't have cooled 'em off any if you know what I mean.

But she didn't talk back. She looked up at me, hesitantly, seemingly on the point of speaking, then took a quick look around as though to make sure that no one was listening.

"Tommy," she said softly—very, very softly. "There won't be any lineup over here on payday. No one will be over here but me."

"Now, that makes a lot of sense," I said. "Six hundred men with fourteen days' pay in their pocket, and. . . ."

"There won't be."

"Won't be?" I said. "Won't be what? Well?" I waited, frowning. "There's six hundred men on the line. Nothing can change that. And they'll have two weeks made in another six-seven days. So . . . so. . . . Wait a minute!" I said. "Are you telling me that they won't get paid?"

"*Sshh!*" She shot a terrified glance into the darkness. "No! I'm not telling you anything! I haven't told you anything!"

She started to back away from me, her face very white in

135

the night. I grabbed her by the shoulders, and she tore out of my grasp.

"Leave, Tommy! Go away, you hear?"

"But . . . but. . . ."

"I'll follow you later. I swear I will! I'll write you general delivery in Fort Worth or Dallas or. . . . But you've got to leave now. Please, honey! *Please!*"

"No," I said. "I'm staying."

"But you can't! You just can't!"

I told her she'd darned sure see if I couldn't; whenever I left she'd be going right along with me. She pleaded with me a little longer and then she called me a darned old stubborn fool and said I could do whatever I doggoned pleased, but I'd better not come near her again.

"I don't like you, Tommy Burwell! I never did like you! You're just as mean and hateful as you can be, and I wouldn't go to a dogfight with you. An' . . . an' you ever come near me again, I'll just slap you good!"

"I'll look forward to it," I said. "See you tomorrow night."

I turned and walked away from her. She ran after me a few steps, scolding and pleading and finally crying. But I kept right on heading for camp, not daring to turn around for fear I'd weaken and give in to her. And three-four minutes later I heard the slam of the housecar doors as she locked herself in for the night.

There was a kind of grim finality about it. A don't-forget-I-warned-you sound. It slowed me down for a moment, forced me to think of what I might be getting myself into. If I hadn't talked-up so big to her and if I hadn't been a chronic hard-head, I just might have done what she'd begged me to do.

But I had and I was, so I didn't. Instead, I went right on into camp.

A light was burning in the high-pressure tent, and I could see a shadow moving against the wall. Otherwise, everyone appeared to be bedded down. Or everyone, that is, but Wingy Warfield. He was out fooling around the wash benches, trying to find something wrong, I figured, so he could bellow about it.

I remembered how he'd knocked me to the law, making it look like I had a death-grudge against Bud Lassen just because I hadn't shaken hands with him. A real nice guy, Wingy was— risking my neck just for the fun of hearing himself loud-mouth! Apparently, he remembered, too, and he naturally thought I'd be sore, because he was sure one nervous camp boss as I came up to him.

I put a big smile on my face and slapped him on the back. "How are you, Wingy, my friend," I said. "How's it goin', old pal?"

"H-How . . . *friend?*" he said. "P-Pal?"

"You know it," I said. "You can't fool me, Wingy. The law told me all the nice things you said about me. Why, I'll bet I'd be in jail yet if it wasn't for you."

I squeezed a five-dollar bill into his hand; told him he'd just have to take it or I'd be sore. After all, he'd saved my life, and friends were supposed to help each other.

"W-Well . . . well, Jesus, Tommy!" He let out a long deep breath, somehow managing to stick out his chest and look cocky. "By God, that's damned white of you, boy! Ain't nothin' like a real friend, I always say, an' any time you need anything you just tell ol' Wingy Warfield!"

"That's my pal!" I gave him another slap on the back. "By the way, pal, some guys came in from town about an hour and a half, two hours ago. Three guys with beards. I wonder if you happened to. . . ."

"You mean the guys that witnessed for you?" he cut in on me. "Those three?"

"Wit . . . what?" I said.

"You know, the guys that cleared you. The three that saw Bud Lassen get hisself killed."

And the three that had been with Carol!

"Yes," I said. "Those are the ones I'm talking about. Do you know what tents they're in?"

He said, o' course, he knew. There was damned little that went on in camp that Wingy Warfield didn't know! "Longden's in number three tent, Bigger's in four and Goss is in seven. I reckon they're all asleep by now, but. . . ."

"Burwell!"

It was Higby. He came striding toward me, jaw set, swinging a pick handle in his hand. Wingy Warfield took a quick look at him, then at me, and scooted away from his ol' pal Tommy Burwell just as fast as his big flat feet could take him.

I lighted a cigarette, casually flipping the match away as Higby strode up.

"Yeah?" I said. "Want something?"

"You were told not to come back here, Burwell. Now, let's see you make tracks!"

"But I've been cleared," I said. "You know that. Why can't I have a job?"

"We've got no jobs for birds like you! You've made nothing

138

but trouble since you hit camp and, by God, you're not making any more!"

"I don't plan on making any trouble," I said. "I never make trouble when I can make money."

"Beat it!" He pointed with the pick handle. "Get your ass long-gone or you'll be digging this Irish toothpick out of it!"

I drawled that I reckoned I'd wait for payday. He jerked the pick handle up like a baseball bat, and I repeated the word.

"Payday," I said softly. "Payday, Mr. Higby. I hear it's going to be something pretty special."

It was just a guess. About all I had to go on was what Four Trey had said: That Higby would have no place to go when he wound up here. That this would probably be the last big pipeline to be built.

I was betting a guess against a beating. But the guess apparently was a good one. He lowered the pick handle, wet his lips, hesitantly.

"You're not being smart, Tommy. I don't know where you tie in or how. But the smartest thing you can do is to drop it and beat it."

"I want a job," I said. "What have you got open?"

"Tommy, for God's sake, son . . . !"

"Yeah?" I said. "What did you say you could give me?"

He started to say something else, then brought his mouth shut with a snap. "How does a mormon board suit you, punk?"

"Mormon . . . !" I gulped, tried to make my voice nonchalant. "Fine," I said. "Nothing I like better than riding a mormon board."

"You do, eh?" His eyes slitted grimly. "Like pouring dope, too?"

"Why not?"

"Good," he grunted. "You're going to be doing both."

They were the lousiest jobs on a pipeline. The lousiest jobs in the world. The board killed you, and the dope cooked you.

I wondered if I couldn't have squeezed him for something better and I reckoned I probably could have, *if* I hadn't played right into his hands. He'd used my cockiness against me, leading me into acting the tough guy. Now, I couldn't back down without appearing the punk he'd called me. And it just wasn't in me to do that.

I'd bet into a cold deck and I couldn't pull my chips.

My working partner and I hoisted the mormon board behind the fill from the ditch. We slammed it down hard, forcing its blade flush with the earth. Then, stiff-armed, with all our weight bearing downward on the handles, we signaled to the tractor driver on the other side of the ditch.

He began to back away slowly, taking the slack out of the heavy cable between board and tractor. When it was tight, he poured on the coal, and the tractor roared backward and our board went forward, slowly dumping our load of fill back into the ditch. When it was all in, the tractor slacked off on the cable, allowing us to reset the board for another bite.

It was about six feet long, that board. Six feet long and

maybe three feet deep. Put a plow handle at each end of the top of a kitchen table, and you'll have a pretty good picture of it. Of course, it was built a hell of a lot heavier than any tabletop. Two men had just about all they could do to lift it. But lifting it was the easiest part of the job. The real work was in riding it toward the ditch.

The ditch was treetop deep in some places. A man standing at the bottom of it could just barely clear the top with a long-handled muckstick. Naturally then, you were never pushing a light load of fill. Any bite you took would be a big one, seven or eight hundred pounds of rock and earth. And it fought you every damned inch of the way.

It kicked, it bucked, it tried to ride up over the fill. One side would be pushing rock when the other had only loose dirt. That allowed one end to whip ahead of the other, which meant that it was going to do some tall whipping to whoever was hanging on to it. I almost had a shoulder dislocated my first day on the board. An hour later, the handle kicked back on the guy who was spelling me, and he dragged-up with two broken ribs.

There'd been no spellers after that first day. There just weren't enough men who'd take the job. They'd drag-up before they'd take it. This was my third day on the job, and I'd had five different sets of partners. Looking at the one I had now, I figured I was just about due to have another one.

He was stripped to the waist, his hair tied back pirate fashion with a bandanna. His face was pock-marked from gravel-stings, and his mouth was caked with dusty blood where the board had jumped up at him. There was an ugly heaving to his chest, a losing struggle for breath. The shuddery shaking of it was something to make you a little sick. A mighty shaking, yet somehow too weak to break the sweat-formed crust of mud which encased his naked torso like a cast.

"Take a doss, bo," I told him. "It's not worth it."

He turned glazed eyes toward me; fixed unseeing eyes. "Huh?"

"Let go. Walk away from it," I said.

"Huh?"

I yelled, trying to get through to him. The tractor-driver took it as a signal. The slack went out of the cable, and the board began to move forward. There was nothing to do but grab the handle and ride it.

I didn't ride it long; not more than a couple of seconds. After that I stopped riding and flew.

I soared up into the air, and headed straight down into the ditch. I did a twisting jackknife, managing to get my feet down and my head up. But I couldn't miss the ditch. It was a good thing I didn't, too, because of that mormon board. And it would have cut me in two if I hadn't been out of the way.

I was shook up pretty bad when my feet slammed down on the pipe. But I wasn't really hurt so much as shocked. Someone held a hand down to me, and I climbed back up out of the ditch, spitting dirt and brushing dust from my eyes. I scrambled over the top of the fill and down the other side.

All work had stopped. A cluster of men stood around the sprawled body of my former partner, leaning on their shovels and picks while the straw boss bent over him.

The guy was dead, of course. He'd needed the job too badly to quit, and the board had killed him. The straw boss straightened, turned his head to spurt out a mouthful of tobacco juice. He wiped his mouth with the back of his hand and brushed the hand against the side of his pants.

"That goddam board," he said, in a deep Southwestern drawl. "That board done went and yanked the heart clean out of a fella named Otto Cooper, an' I'll bet me a pretty no one knows a danged thing about him."

No one did.

Higby drove up, wanting to know why the hell the work stoppage, and he had nothing on the guy either. Cooper had hired on late with a bad case of brokes, so naturally he'd gone straight on the mormon board. That was all that was known about him.

Higby drew the straw boss to one side and had a few words with him. Then he drove on down the line, and the straw boss nodded to me.

" 'Bout caught up with the dope gang, Tommy, so we're givin' the old board a rest. Just one more little go-round for you an' me, and then we'll break for lunch."

"I figured," I said. "Let's wrap it up and put a button on it."

He took the dead man's head, and I took his feet. We lowered him into the ditch, spreading him face down against the pipe. We climbed back up again, latched on to the mormon board and signaled the tractor driver.

The board moved forward, pushing its great load of earth into the ditch, burying the body of Otto Cooper beneath it.

The straw boss spit tobacco juice down wind. He squinted at the straight-up sun, wiping a hand against the mouth, wiping the hand against his pants. "Son-of-a-bitch," he drawled. "Shit and three are nine. Well, he's sure as hell got the world's longest grave, ain't he?"

"He'll have company before we make the Gulf," I said. "A lot of company."

"Ain't it the truth, now?" He nodded solemnly. "Ain't that the God's truth? Well, screw and two is four and frig makes ten. An' here comes the chow truck."

The chow truck parked a ways up-line near the largest gang of workmen. I took my time about getting to it, needing to get the kinks out of my arms and back as much as I needed food and wanting to avoid the jostling I'd get in a crowd.

The flunky loaded my tray and filled my coffee bowl. I looked around for a good spot to sit, finally hunkering down away from everyone on a joint of line pipe. It wasn't a prize place to eat, as it turned out. The dope-boiler was a little too close, and its pale thin smoke stung me like a swarm of ants.

I went on eating, trying to tough it out; just too tired and sore to move. Finally, though, I couldn't take it any longer, and I started to get up.

"You just stay there." A foot came down on top of mine. "You just stay right there, Tommy, boy."

I said, "What the . . ." And tried to lunge upward. I couldn't do it, of course, with my foot pinned down, and I banged back down on the pipe.

"Now, that's better, Tommy, boy. Not a real good spot to squat, it seems like, but this won't take long."

He was one of the bearded men I'd seen last night. He squatted down in front of me, his eyes dancing with malicious amusement. As he did so, the two other men I'd seen sat down on the pipe with me. One on each side, squeezed in close.

"I'm Longden." The first man pointed a thumb at himself. "Those two gents are Bigger and Doss, and if you'd've asked us who we were instead of Wingy Warfield we'd've told you so. Real polite about answering questions, ain't we, boys?"

"That's us. The best little old question-answerers in the world."

"That's good," I said, trying to keep the shakes out of my voice. "Then I reckon you won't mind telling me why you had to have your arms twisted before you admitted seeing Lassen get killed."

"What makes you think they were twisted, Tommy, boy?"

"A friend of mine as good as said so," I said, and I told him how Four Trey had known they were clearing me before they did it. "He found out that you were out of camp that night and he threatened to talk if you didn't."

Longden pursed his lips, exchanged a glance with the other two—a signal—and said I had it all wrong.

"Now, here's the way it was, Tommy, boy. Here's exactly the way it was. In the first place, Bud Lassen didn't just *get* killed. We killed him . . ."

"Wha . . . !" I stared at him. "You . . . you admit it?"

"Why not? Talk never hurt anyone without proof to back

it up." He chuckled softly. "Being sound of mind and body, as the saying is, we naturally thought Bud was ripe for killin'. He was a bum who could be trouble, and you were building into a nuisance. So we figured to kill him and stick you for it. We like to do things that way, Tommy, boy. Plan a killing so it either looks like an accident or points the finger at someone else."

"That's the way," Doss nodded. "We made it an accident with nosy ol' Bones, so you had to be chumped for murderin' Bud."

"Right," Bigger said. "You got to switch 'em around, you know, because too many accidents is as bad as an unsolved murder."

Longden beamed at them like an admiring father. "Good boys. Aren't they good boys, Tommy? Well, anyway. It was Carol that twisted our arms, not Four Trey. He told her what had happened to you, and she did the rest. Swore she wouldn't go through with some plans we had, unless we got you out of the clink."

He spoke as idly as though he were discussing the weather. We were within fifty feet of hundreds of men, yet these three, these three killers . . .

"You're going to hold up the payroll," I said. "Carol is going to drive the escape car."

"And she'll get a nice cut of the loot, Tommy, boy. Plenty for the two of you to set up housekeeping on. That's what you want, ain't it?" His brows quirked in cynical amusement. "Me and the boys certainly have no objection, do we, boys?"

Doss said he certainly didn't object, and Bigger said that

he was all for it. I added up to an all-right guy in his book, and a girl just didn't get no better than Carol!

"You see, Tommy, boy?" Longden spread his hands expressively. "We're all for you livin' happily ever after, an' so on. But right now you're going to have to keep away from her. We've got plans to make and work to do and we can't have you hangin' around."

He gave me an amiable tap on the knee by way of emphasis. I tried to jerk away from him, and the other two held me where I was.

"Why . . . why, damn you!" I sputtered. "What kind of punk do you think I am? You think you can just walk up to me and tell me what I can do an' what I can't do and make me like it? I'll see Carol whenever I damned well please, and. . . ."

"Huh-uh. No, you won't, Tommy, boy. Not unless you can see when you're dead."

"Big deal! And what's Carol going to say about you killing me? You get tough with me, and she'll blow the deal on you."

"She might, Tommy. She just might—if she knew about it. But, of course, she ain't going to. No one is."

"Like hell! I just disappear and no one thinks anything of it? Now that makes a lot of sense!"

Longden said that it sure did, didn't it, and Bigger beamed that I sure caught on fast. Show me which end of a match to strike and I'd figure it out in no time. Doss said that a boy as bright as me prob'ly had to hide under the bed in the morning so that folks could see the sun come up.

"Y'see, here's the way it is, Tommy, boy," Longden

continued. "Carol's begged you to leave. Three-four people have, everyone that gives a dang about you. That's the way it is, right? Carol an' everyone else has done everything they could to point you away from here an' start you to movin'. . . ."

"But . . . Well, maybe they did, but. . . ."

"So you don't show up some fine morning, and what do folks think? Why, they just think that Tommy Burwell finally whistled-up the dogs and pissed on the fire and made himself long-gone."

He nodded firmly, waited a moment to see if I had anything else to say. I did have . . . but I wasn't going to say it to him. So he jerked his head at the other two, and the three of them got up and walked away together.

The work whistle blew.

I carried my tray back to the chow truck and headed for the dope gang.

Ditch pipe receives a protective coating in the factory these days and has for a long time past. But in those times, the coating was applied at the ditch. As with blasting, it was the quickest way of doing it and, above all, the cheapest. In a different state with a different kind of economy, it would never have been allowed. But in Texas, a state largely dependent on cattle, cotton and oil, practically anything went.

Cotton required large amounts of cheap, backbreaking labor. You could no more farm cotton under healthful conditions than you could raise cattle without men who spent endless hours in the saddle in all kinds of weather, risking their health and their lives for a pittance, growing old when they were young. So also with the oil industry and those related to it.

There were no absolutely safe jobs in the oil fields. They ranged from fairly safe to downright hazardous. To have made them completely safe would have been too costly, it was reasoned, and the industry could not be hampered in any way. On the contrary, the state's attitude was fiercely protective.

Texas oil men complained that the Standard Oil Company was unfair competition. So for many years Standard was barred from the state by law. It could operate everywhere else in the world, but not in Texas. Anything or anyone who made trouble for Texas industry was buying trouble for himself. And that included people who did the unhealthy, dirty and dangerous jobs of that industry.

They didn't *have* to do 'em, did they? No one forced them to. They knew what they were getting into when they hired out, and if they didn't want to risk it they didn't have to take it!

Insurance? Sure, there was insurance. But insurance was a big industry, too, and fully deserving of the state's protection. You couldn't expect an insurance company to sell (or an employer to buy) policies on workmen in certain kinds of jobs. Not unless those policies were so restricted and qualified as to make them virtually worthless. It would cost too much; it would cut profits. Costs had to be held down, profits held up.

Which takes us back to me and the dope gang.

There were three men in the gang, plus a straw boss who checked the pipe after it was doped. One man walked on each side of the ditch, each holding one end of a hammocklike device. This was wrapped one turn around the pipe, and held loosely to form a kind of apron underneath. The third man, me, poured the dope into this apron.

I used a pouring can pretty much like the sprinkling can you'd use in your garden, but with the spray-nozzle removed. As I poured, the other two men pulled the hammock back and forth in a sawing motion, coating the pipe with a thin layer of liquid asphalt.

The hammock men could keep pretty well out of the way of the fumes. I had to stoop right into them. They walked forward. I had to walk backward to keep out of their way.

I wore goggles, of course; I also kept my hat jammed low and my collar turned up and a bandanna tied across my face like a Western outlaw. But that was all I could do, and it wasn't even halfway enough. In the time that I poured dope—that afternoon plus two days more—my face was burned so badly that the skin hung in strips. My neck and forehead weren't much better off, either, and I think my eyesight would have been permanently damaged in a very little while longer.

It was a tough world, the Far West Texas of the twenties. You might not live through it and you might not look pretty if you did, but people would know you were a man from a mile away.

At the end of two and a half days, the pipe was doped as far as it was welded, and Higby curtly told me that I could go back to shooting powder if Four Trey would have me. I braced Whitey for it, all nervous and edgy and on the defensive because he hadn't even spoken to me since I'd been back. He still didn't speak, either.

He just listened, then shook his head and turned away without answering. I grabbed him and whirled him back around.

"Now . . . n-now you listen to me!" I stammered, my voice cracking with fury. "You just l-listen to me, Four Trey Whiteside! I'm twenty-one years old and I'm a man. You keep poking it at me that I am! I'm a man, I've got to make my own life, and you make me know it. But the minute I start to do it you slap me down. You. . . ."

"I do it for your own good!"

"How do you know it is? What have you done with your own life that makes you know what's good for me? Who the hell do you think you are, anyway? Do you think you're God? Are you God, Mr. Four Trey Whitey?"

He said, "Now, listen to me, Tommy!" And I asked for how long should I listen. How long would he tell me what to do and give a damn whether I did it or not.

"A day, an hour, a minute? You play the father, the big brother, only when you take a notion to. And what happens if I start playing my part? That's another story, isn't it? Then you freeze up fast. I'm told to get back where I belong. To go my own way and not bother you. One minute you're my father and the next you don't know me. You . . ."

I stormed away at him, about as near to crying as a man gets. I needed a friend, a real friend, because I was all mixed up over Carol and the mess I'd walked into. I was scared and worried and I didn't know what to do or where to turn, and he . . . he. . . .

His face softened. He looked down at the ground uneasily, guiltily, and I think he spoke to me several times before he finally got my attention.

"Tommy . . . I'm sorry, Tommy. You go back on powder with me in the morning."

"Well, you ought to be sorry!" I said. "You . . . An' you don't have to take me back on powder if you don't want me! I'm a man and I've got pride, an'. . . ."

"And I've still got half a pint in my bindle. And you and I are goin' to put it where it'll do the most good!"

We did, and we made a lot of talk in the course of doing it. Rather, he talked, and I mostly listened.

". . . some people are afraid of caring, Tommy. They're afraid of letting anyone get too close to them. Because when they do care, they care too much. They put all their eggs in one basket, as the saying is, and when something happens to the basket. . . ." He shook his head, staring off into space. "It almost kills them, Tommy. It almost killed me when I lost my wife. For a long time, I wished that it would, but instead. . . ."

"I'm sorry," I said. "I shouldn't have talked up to you the way I did."

"Yes, you should have, Tommy. It made me see something that I hadn't seen before, and I needed to see it. You can't live another person's life for him. If you care for him, you've got to do it on his terms for what he is, not yours for what you think he should be. Now, in my book you were dead wrong to come back here. I'm convinced of it. But...."

"I had to, Four Trey. I just *had* to!"

"You did," he nodded. "And who am I to act like you're not worth spitting on because you did? If you're for someone, you're for 'em come hell or high water. If you lose someone you care deeply about, well, at least you had 'em for a while. You're still 'way ahead of the game and you've got no call to stop playing. You loved someone and they loved you, just as each of you was—good, bad and indifferent—the only way to love. Because you were people, not gods, and you didn't make demands that it wasn't in the other fellow to meet. And you were richer for having loved, for even a little while...."

That's about how our conversation ended. With both of us understanding things we hadn't understood before, and better friends than we'd ever been.

It was on the tip of my tongue to tell him about Longden and his two bearded buddies, but I didn't want to push things too far just when we'd gotten on a solid footing. Anyway, we'd have plenty of opportunities to talk now that we'd be working together again.

As it turned out, I didn't have to tell him. Because Longden hadn't been kidding when he'd warned me to stay away from Carol or get killed.

But that's getting ahead of the story. I've gotten a couple days ahead of it in telling about getting square with Four Trey, so let's move back a little.

Back to the end of my first afternoon on the dope gang . . .

Higby had been driving hard, and the line had been moving right along, and the job was now almost an hour's ride from camp. Going in that night, the guy riding next to me on the flatbed remarked that we'd have to be moving camp soon, jumping it south maybe twenty-five or thirty miles, because the ride was taking too much time. I nodded without speaking, trying to save my cracked and blistered lips as much as possible.

I could hardly bear soap and water for washing that night and I sort of groaned with every bite of the hot chow. In the long run, of course, stretching the burned skin was good for it. Or a lot better, anyway, then letting it tighten on you like a blistered mask. It helped it, if you could stand it, and after dinner I smeared it good with butter, and that helped, too.

The cook watched me sympathetically, cursing the "goddam capitalists." He said hell was too cold for such people, and, come the revolution, they'd all get their butts warmed with a cutting torch so they'd know how it felt to cook a man alive. Then he threw a thirty-pound ham in the garbage and gave me a four-ounce bottle of jake (Jamaica ginger) to ease me through the night.

The old crumb boss in my tent hovered around me for a long time, wanting to do things for me and letting me know he was sorry. Finally, I pretended to go to sleep, and he went to his own bunk and sacked in. When everyone else had done the same and the camp was dark, I slipped out the back of the tent and headed for town.

I'd never felt less like walking five miles in my life. But there was no phone short of town, and I had to phone Sheriff Darrow. I'd have walked five thousand miles to help Carol, and this was the only way I could do it.

I knew she couldn't have been mixed up in anything before. She just wasn't old enough. She was only taking part in the payroll robbery because she was forced to, but that wouldn't cut any ice with the law. If you commit a crime you're a criminal and you can't clear yourself by claiming that you were forced to commit it. So the robbery had to be stopped before it started, and Darrow was the only one who could do it.

There was a booth phone next to the garage, and I called him from there. He wasn't at his office, late as it was, but I managed to reach him at home. In the background, I could hear a baby crying faintly and a few words of a woman's voice complaining about people who were always late for dinner. I didn't hear very much of it, because there was a sound like a door being closed, then an amused chuckle from him as he told me to go ahead.

I started talking. After a minute or so he broke in on me.

"Those fellows are teasing you, Burwell. It may be that they don't want you hanging around their sister, or their foster sister, I should say. But the rest is nonsense."

"Nonsense!" I said. "They've already killed two people and they threaten to kill me, an'. . . ."

"They haven't killed anyone. Both deaths were accidents."

"The heck they were! You . . . you just don't know 'em sheriff! You don't know. . . ."

"Yes, I do, Burwell," he said quietly. "I know everything there is to know about those men. Information is a big part of my job, and I'm very good at getting it. But in their case I didn't have to. They came in and identified themselves the moment they entered my county."

"B-But. . . ." I stared into the phone wordlessly. "But, dammit. . . ."

"They're the Long brothers. *The* Long brothers, understand? I'll admit they probably bought their pardons; they've done it before. But they claim to be going straight now and they certainly act like they mean to. I think they've proved that by coming in to see me in the beginning and coming forward later to clear you."

"You do, huh?" I laughed shakily. "The worst killers and crooks in Texas, and you think . . . !" I choked up for a moment, unable to go on. "Don't you see, sheriff? They knew you'd find out who they were, anyway, so they played smart and beat you to the punch. And they didn't clear me until they had to. Carol found out what. . . ."

He sighed, cutting in on me again. "You told me, Burwell. You told me. I hold no brief for the Longs—Longie, that's Longden, or Bigger or Doss. I've got no use for any of 'em. I don't like what they're letting a potentially nice girl make of herself, but they're not wanted anywhere now, and I'm not running a Sunday school. So unless. . . ."

"What about that car?" I said. "Why, sheriff, if you'd just . . . !"

"What about it? This is a bad part of the world to have a breakdown in. A smart person keeps his car in first-class condition."

"But it's *more* than that! It's a, uh, well, it's a get-away car if I've ever seen one!"

"Well, now, of course, that's different! How many have you seen, Burwell?"

He waited; laughed teasingly. I said a few things that weren't very nice, and he sobered and said he was sorry.

"You've had a bad time, Burwell. When a man goes to the trouble that you have to do the right thing, he deserves something better than to be laughed at. I was afraid there'd be trouble if you went back there. The Longs are notorious for dead-pan kidding. Even if they didn't indulge in it there was always the chance you'd find out who they were, and get the wind up because of the girl. Now, if you'll take my advice. . . ."

"Wait!" I said. "Wait a minute, sheriff! I just remembered something else."

"Did you?" He stifled a yawn. "Well?"

"Higby. He's in on the robbery. Why, I just dropped a little hint that there was something screwy about payday, and. . . ."

"*Burwell!*" His voice was suddenly curt. "Have you been popping off any around camp about this?"

"Of course not," I said. "Why would I do a thing like that?"

"Because you seem to be about as brainless as a man can get! Higby has a pipeline to build within a certain amount of time. There are enormous penalties to pay for every day he runs over that time, and a whopping bonus for every day

157

he's under. He had to do the job and he has to do it without a hitch, and what kind of men does he have to do it with?"

"Now, look," I said. "I. . . ."

"He has to do it with scum, Burwell! That's what they are, mostly. Hoboes, bums, drunks and jailbirds—the scum of the oil fields. Men who make a career out of finding reasons for *not* working. Now just what do you think would happen if some lovesick, loudmouth kid hinted that something might happen to their pay? Well? My guess is that he wouldn't have enough men left to build a barn."

"But I didn't say that much to Higby! I didn't hint that. . . ."

"Practically anything you said would have given him a jolt. You see, he knows who the Longs are. They were hired on at my suggestion."

"H-He *knows?*" I said. "You suggested it? Why . . . why, that's crazy!"

Darrow sighed that if I was halfway as smart as I thought I was I'd see it differently. The Longs had no honest skill, and the pipeline was the county's major employer of unskilled labor. By seeing that they were hired on, they could not only be kept track of—their whereabouts known at all times—but helped to earn a living instead of stealing it.

"Both the pipeline company and I could rest more comfortably by having them there. What we didn't count on was you and that girl falling for each other, which naturally was one hell of a big hazard. Because if she ever got confidential with you, a romantic knothead with all his brains in his crotch. . . ."

My face was burning, and not just from the dope either. I said, all right, maybe I was a knothead. But he could do one thing at least without upsetting anyone's applecart.

"Just move in and take Carol away from there, sheriff. If you'll do that. . . ."

"I won't. I'm not in the business of rousting whores. If I were, I couldn't legally do anything until she actually started turning tricks."

He made sounds of hanging up. I yelled that I'd bet he was in on the robbery himself, and if he wouldn't do his job I'd call someone who would.

He snapped that what I'd do was go back to camp and keep my mouth shut, and if I didn't do it he'd break one of his own rules and float me out of the county.

"One more thing, Burwell. You tell the Longs for me that I'm pretty good at joking myself, and I'll give 'em a sample of it if there's any more talk about killing or robberies!"

There was a sharp *click* as he broke the connection.

I sorted through my change, found enough to call the Matacora county attorney. He was expecting it, having just received a call from Darrow.

"Burwell, huh?" he grunted. "What you been drinking, boy? Speak up, dammit! A man ought to lay off the stuff if he can't handle it."

"I'm not drunk!" I said. "I haven't had a damn thing! All I. . . ."

"Well, drink something, then. Get your mind off of gals for a while. That's your trouble, Burwell. Thinkin' about gals instead of drinkin'. Worst thing in the world for a man."

"Please," I begged. "If you'll just listen to me, sir. . . ."

"No time, boy. No time. Now sober up and you'll feel a hell of a lot better in the morning."

He hung up.

So did I. Baffled, frustrated, confused, hardly knowing whether to bawl or laugh.

I came out of the booth and stood there in the night for a moment, letting the cooling wind wash over my face.

Darrow had had an answer for everything: about Higby, the Longs, Carol—everything. And all his answers were logical. What he'd said made a hell of a lot more sense than what I'd said. It didn't actually, but it seemed to.

How could anyone believe that Longden hadn't been kidding? That he wasn't just having some fun with a green kid? How could anyone believe that he'd tell me he was going to commit a robbery if he really intended to do it?

The fact was, of course, that he'd told me because he'd had to.

What I'd gotten out of Carol had pointed me toward the truth. Higby's reaction to my payday hint had just about wrapped it up. All I needed was to think on it a little and I'd be running to the sheriff. So Longden had done the only thing he could do. And I'd walked right into the trap.

Darrow was smart. If I'd only told him what I suspected and why, the odds were that he would have seen things as I did, and the Longs would have been jailed and Carol would have been free. But instead of just telling him what I'd *suspected,* I'd told him what Longden had told me, and when Darrow had laughed and teased me about it. . . .

Of course, he'd laughed! Who wouldn't? I should have

laughed with him, agreed that it did sound crazy while pointing out just how smart that craziness was. If I'd only done
that, behaving reasonably and sensibly instead of losing my
temper and shouting and calling him a crook—but I hadn't
done that.

I'd acted like a fool. I'd acted like one, and he'd treated
me like one.

I winced, remembering; realizing that I'd washed myself
up with the only people who could have helped. I could never
turn to them again, no matter what happened, no matter what
the Longs did. I'd lost Carol for all time, and it was my own
damned fault. I felt so low-down miserable and mad at myself
that I groaned out loud.

*"Dammit! Dammit to hell, anyway! How stupid can a guy
get?"*

"Now, don't you feel bad about it, Tommy boy." Longden
ambled out of the shadows surrounding the booth. "C'mon
and I'll give you a lift back to camp."

The car, Carol's housecar, was parked behind one of the
town's abandoned buildings. Longden drove cross-lots until
he was out of town and had picked up the rutted trail into
camp. He kept the lights off, the motor merely purring as it
raced. We slid through the night like phantoms, the black car
almost invisible, virtually silent.

"A real good wagon, ain't she, Tommy, boy?" Longden

chuckled proudly. "What do you figure she cost us, huh? Just make a guess."

"I don't give a damn," I said. "Where's Carol?"

"Why, she's just fine, Tommy, boy. Got some fellas keepin' an eye on her while I'm out dry-runnin'. Don't you ever worry about Carol, Tommy. There ain't no time that we ain't got someone lookin' out for her."

"How?" I said. "By giving her black eyes? Slapping her around?"

"Aw, naw. O' course not. That ain't hardly ever been necessary. It's a lot easier an' nicer just to keep her broke and have her watched. And we don't always have to do the watchin'; not as long as she knows that someone just *might* be doin' it."

"Yeah, sure," I said. "You're real smart, you are."

It wasn't any compliment the way I meant it, but it was the truth. When it came to thinking up new angles in crime, the Longs—particularly, Longie—were in a class by themselves. The setup of the gang itself was unlike that of any other gang.

Back in the beginning, before they'd had a gang, the Longs had gotten themselves so well-known that it was just about impossible for them to conceal their identity. So they no longer made much of an effort to. Instead, they made sure that no member of the gang was ever recognized or caught.

Most gang bosses stayed safely in the background, sometimes taking no part in a job except for the planning. But the Longs were out in front every step of the way, keeping their gang members in the background. And no one ever knew how many were in the gang, because it wasn't always apparent who *was* in it.

A member of the gang might be in the place being robbed disguised as a workman. Or he might turn out to be a "customer" or a passerby. The Longs only pulled big jobs, ones upward of fifty thousand dollars. It would always be a bank job or the payroll of a big factory, or something of the kind. A place with a lot of people around. One of those people, almost any one of 'em, might belong to the gang. And he'd have you dead at the first wrong move you made.

It had been a hell of a long time since anyone had made a move against the gang during a holdup. For all anyone knew, they might have given up their hidden-man technique, but no one took the only way of finding out. You don't have to convince people very often when you do it by killing.

The Long brothers had gone to prison several times. They could afford to; just as quickly as they were in and out. But the gang remained on the outside, every man of them. Tremendously loyal to the brothers, raising huge sums of money for them; functioning like a well-oiled machine through their years of working together.

And now, at last, the Longs had blundered. It wouldn't help Carol, but they had made one heck of a mistake in tackling the robbery of the pipeline payroll.

"Yeah, Tommy, boy?" The car was slowing, coming to a stop. "Yeah?" Longden turned in the seat and grinned at me. "Got somethin' troubling you?"

"You're going to have something troubling *you*," I said. "You and everyone in your gang is."

"Gang? What makes you think we got a gang, Tommy?"

"Because I'm not stupid. There's six hundred men in camp—*six hundred!* And they're not the sort to sit and twiddle their thumbs while someone walks off with their pay. It'll take a dozen armed men to handle 'em, and they won't have any gravy train doing it!"

"Well, now, gee whiz, by ding!" he drawled. "You seen right through me, Tommy, boy. But what about this trouble we're supposed to get into? Where's that supposed to come in?"

I said the trouble was going to be in the getaway, and he raised his brows, putting on as though he was puzzled. He said he'd thought they had everything planned pretty perfect, but maybe he'd better run through it from the beginning.

"We got this car, now, a car that can just about stand up on its hind legs and turn handsprings. And we got me drivin' it, comes getaway time. And you see how I drive, Tommy, boy; how I learn the area so well around a job that I can drive it in the dark with the lights off. I always do that, y'know, Tommy. I do it even when I don't have to, because a fella just never knows when havin' to is. He might have to, without knowin' that he does, y'know? But mainly it's a test. It's a way of making sure that I've got the whole area laid out in my mind, every little twist and turn and bump. The *only* way. If I can drive it in the dark. . . ."

"I get your point," I said. "Go on."

"Well, then, there's Carol. We kept her out of things her whole life, sent her away to school and all an' treated her fine, just savin' her for something special like this. So no one has ever big-eyed her. No one knows that she ain't just what she appears to be, a hustler makin' a pipeline. She's been there all along, and now everyone's used to her. An' no one ever figures that she's totin' guns and ammunition, an'. . . ."

"Go on," I said. "Get to something I don't know. You pull the robbery, and then what?"

"Why, we just take off, that's what. Just like we always do."

"But there's a big difference this time. This time you'll all be exposed. The law will be looking for all of you, instead of just you and your brothers. When you're caught, there'll be no one on the outside to work for you and raise money."

He nodded solemnly. Too solemnly to mean it. "Yeah, Tommy. But you said we'd have trouble gettin' away."

"That's the trouble. In *having* to get away. All of you, I mean. You'll all have to leave the country or get caught."

"So what's the problem? This here car'll carry a dozen men as easy as apples, an' we're sittin' right on the doorstep of Mexico."

He nodded again, eyes twinkling. Looking as solemn as all get-out. I said he knew damned well what I meant, so why pretend that he didn't?

"Now, Tommy, boy," he drawled. "Now, that ain't nice, Tommy. Here you are practically a member of the family and you've sort of taken on the job of reportin' us to the sheriff an'. . . . Why would I joke a fine, upstanding, young fella like you?"

"Forget it. To hell with you," I said.

"Tell you what I'll do, Tommy. You square me away on what this problem is, an' I'll let you see Carol. You can be alone with her for, oh, three or four hours. Okay?"

"Knock it off," I said. "You wouldn't dare let me go near her. If she knew I was still here and intended to stay, you wouldn't be able to kill me like you've threatened. And that threat is the only hold you have over us."

He said it made him feel plumb bad to hear me talk that way. Danged if it didn't sound just like I didn't trust him or somethin'.

"C'mon an' tell me, Tommy, boy," he wheedled. "What have you got to lose, anyway? I figure you got somethin' plenty important to say, an' I'm willing to pay the price to hear it!"

"Well. . . ." I hesitated, studying him. Certain that he was lying but hoping that he wasn't. Wanting to see Carol so bad that I would have believed anything.

"I'm tellin' the God's truth, Tommy." He held up a hand as though swearing. "You just show me where the problem is, an' I'll let you see Carol."

I said, yeah, sure he would. Maybe he'd let me *start* to see her, but I'd get killed on the way. He pointed out casually that he'd hardly go through all that trouble when he could kill me right then and there if he wanted to.

"Not that I do want to, Tommy, boy. I would if I had to, but it ain't somethin' I'm anxious for. The sheriff knows you're stickin' here, no matter what, so if he should come lookin' for you. . . ." He spread his hands expressively. "Now c'mon an' tell me, boy. You do me a favor, an' I'll do you one."

I told him what the problem was.

He waited, watching me interestedly. "Yeah, Tommy?"

"What do you mean, yeah?" I said. "That's it."

"What's it?"

"What I just told you, dammit!"

"Yeah? Maybe you better spell it out for me."

"But . . . ! All right," I said. "It's a big payroll. One heck of a pile of money. But it isn't much when it has to be your last job. It's not nearly enough for a dozen men who have to spend the rest of their lives in a foreign country."

"Yeah?"

"Of course, it isn't. You'd need twice that much, anyway!"

"Yeah?"

"To hell with you!" I said. "I've told you about umpteen times already, and you just sit there saying, yeah! You're not deaf, are you? Well? What's the matter with you, anyway?"

"Just lonesome, Tommy. Just dyin' for amusin' company. Y' know, this is a plumb hard life I lead, boy. Workin' day and night, you might say, doin' the same thing over and over. So when a real amusin' fella like you comes along. . . . What's the matter, Tommy? You ain't sore at me just because I can't see where the problem is?"

I gritted my teeth. I said, all right, I'd go through it one more time.

"You Longs and your men have to live in Mexico the rest of your lives. You can't operate down there and you can't come back here. All right then. The men will be paid for two weeks' work, plus overtime. Some draw very big pay, some middling, some—most of 'em—bottom scale. Averaging them all up, it figures out to, well. . . ."

"Call it a little better than a hundred a piece, Tommy.

167

Maybe sixty-five, seventy thousand for the lot. So what's the problem?"

"The problem," I said slowly, like I was talking to a four-year-old kid. "The problem is that it's not enough money. You need a minimum of twice that much! Now, do you finally understand that? Have you finally got it through your thick skull?"

"We-el. . . ." He scratched his head. "Well, I understand that part, Tommy. I can see that, all right. But there's one leetle thing I don't understand."

"What's that?" I said. "What don't you understand?"

"What the problem is. . . ."

. . . He was still whooping with laughter as I slammed out of the car and started walking toward camp.

As I've said, that took place at the end of my first afternoon on the dope gang. And two nights later, as I've said, Four Trey and I had our talk and patched things up between us.

We'd gone out on the prairie to talk, and I remained there a while after he'd sauntered back to his tent. It was nice there. The wind came to me across hundreds of miles of unobstructed prairie, so clean and sweet smelling. After inhaling dope fumes all day, I couldn't get enough of it.

The sun went down, and dusky-dark came on. I pushed myself up from the grass and went back to my tent. I started thinking about Carol again—or still, I should say, because I never really stopped thinking about her. I sat on the edge of my bunk, the nighttime glooms settling over me, wishing that I was to hell and gone from here and that Carol was with me.

The tent was noisy. It always was at this time of evening, but with payday right on top of us—the day after tomorrow—it was worse than ever. Everyone seemed to be grab-assing or talking at the top of his lungs. Everyone was full of piss and high spirits, planning on how he was going to poop off his dough.

A stiff threw a handful of orange peelings at me. I jumped up, ready to poke him one. Then decided to let it go as he laughed and waved to me. He wanted to know if I'd be dealing blackjack again. I said, "What did he think?" And he laughed again and said he was all set to pin my ears back.

I took off my shoes and lay down on the bunk, turning my back so that everyone would know I wanted to be left alone. The guys nearest me took the hint and moved their racket up toward the front of the tent, and I went back to thinking about Carol.

There was only one thing to do, as I saw it. Since no one would help me, no one would get her away from the Longs, I'd have to do it myself.

How, I didn't know. I didn't have the faintest idea. If I could get to see her, to talk to her, there was a good chance of getting her safely away. We could just fade out into the prairie, and if you really wanted to lose yourself in that prairie, you were just as good as lost. Why, hell, you get could lost mighty easy *without* wanting to, and people could look forever without finding you.

We could escape on foot or, with luck, we could make it in the car. Get to someplace where the law knew their business, instead of being like Darrow, and we'd have a happy ol' time together from then on out. Anyway, I was pretty sure we'd be all right, once I got to her. But how in heck was I going to do that?

How could I get to see her with the Longs watching all the time?

The way I figured, I'd never get but one chance. If I tried and ran into them that would wrap it up and put a button on it. I'd disappear, and no one would ever know but what I'd just decided to take off.

Maybe there'd be some tall wondering about it; some questions asked. But no one could prove anything, and I'd still be dead. So. . . .

Above the racket of the tent, I heard the sudden roar of a flatbed. Then another and another. From outside there was a rising clamor of voices, with Higby's crisp peremptory voice rising above them.

I rolled over on my bunk and sat up. Higby threw back the flap of the tent and looked in; hard of face, cold eyes sweeping from one man to another.

"All right." He began to point, singling out one man after another and gesturing them curtly outside. "All right, swarm out of here! Move, goddammit! Leave your bags and grab your rags!"

They got up uncertainly, wonderingly. There was a rumble of complaint, of questions: What the hell was up, anyway? Higby said to swarm out and find out.

"You back there!" he pointed. "What the frig are you

waiting on? And you and you and you! By Christ, if I have to tell you again . . . !"

His eyes rested on me, my burned and puffy face. They passed over me, and he turned and went back through the flap.

Grumbling and cursing, the men poured out of the tent. I put on my shoes and moved up front. Stood looking out into the night.

Men were loading up on the flatbeds. As fast as one was loaded, it pulled away from camp, motor roaring, and headed up-line. In all there were four of them—four truckloads of men.

Seated side by side on the last truck were the Long brothers.

"Got out of it, huh, Tommy?" It was Wingy Warfield. "Well, you ought to, pal, you ought to. Bad enough to burn a man's face off without working his ass off."

I asked him what the story was, and he told me in his know-it-all way. He'd warned them, he said (whoever "them" was), he'd warned 'em that you couldn't make a deep ditch out here without shoring. Because any damned fool knew that wherever you found a lot of blackjack and scrub-oak, you were going to find water not too far down. Yes, by Jesus, there'd be water-sand, which meant that your ditch would seep on you. And if you didn't have shoring in it . . . !

"Caved in more'n a mile, Tommy. Them poor stiffs is going to be digging out 'til midnight or longer, the way I figure!"

I figured that the way *he* figured wouldn't be more than half-right, but they'd be gone a long time. The Longs would be gone a long time, and an hour was all I needed.

It was a good night for what I had to do. Dark enough for

171

cover, but light enough to let me move right along. I headed across the prairie at a fast walk, and the wind came up at my back, seeming to want to help me along.

I could have done without the wind. It made too much noise as it raked through the grass and scrub brush, keeping my nerves on edge, constantly looking this way and that. Perhaps smothering sounds that I needed to hear.

Because, of course, the Longs weren't my only problem.

The Longs would be tied up for several hours, and possibly the members of their gang would be, too. Possibly Higby had told them to move out with the rest of the work party, and they would have had no choice but to go or get.

The odds were that they'd been drafted along with the others—if they had been in camp. They'd be strong, able-bodied men, naturally, and they'd hired on as unskilled labor. So Higby would have grabbed them, if they'd been there to grab.

But if they'd been out here. . . . If they were out here. . . . Well, then I was in trouble.

And they were, and I was!

How many there were I don't know. But the first one suddenly rose up in front of me when I was less than a quarter-mile out of camp. I whirled around, and there was a guy there, too. He'd come up behind me and now he was almost on top of me. I darted right then left, and still others rose up to head me off.

They closed in, arms outspread, a tightening circle of death. There was no way of getting past them, no way of getting around them. My one hope, a puny one, was to break through them.

172

They came on silently, confidently. Very sure of themselves, a gang of professional killers against one overgrown kid. A rattler couldn't have been surer of a fear-frozen rabbit than they were of me, and I could almost hear their unvoiced laughter.

Ever so slightly, I bent my knees. I drew my leg muscles tight, levered my feet into the dirt and suddenly dived straight ahead.

My head slammed into the guy's guts. He went down, and my momentum shot me over him in a wild somersault. I came to my feet, running. The downed guy groaned and writhed, getting in the way of the others and causing them to stumble and collide. They'd been bunched up, and it had cost them a big advantage. They were no longer a circle of men, just men. And the way to camp was open.

I ran, man, did I ever run! I'd been as good as dead a minute before, but now I was free and running. And I knew they'd never be able to catch me.

They knew it, too, and they didn't even try.

I don't know who threw it—the rock or whatever it was. But the Dodgers could have used him. He was throwing at a moving target in the dark, a throw of almost a hundred feet. But he nailed me like di wa didy.

My whole head seemed to explode. I was out cold before I hit the ground.

During the next hour or so—however long it was—I moved briefly back into consciousness a couple of times. A dim, foggy half-consciousness where everything was blurred and run together and everything that mattered seemed not to matter.

I came to the first time when I bumped into the bottom of some kind of declivity. I couldn't see anyone; probably I didn't even open my eyes. But there was a murmur of voices, blurred and run-together like the rest of my half-conscious world.

Longie warned him. The girl. Stop 'em in the first place. Didn't think they'd tumble f'r each other. Well get the son-of-a-bitch buried.

Something splashed into my face. Dirt. Then more dirt. I began to struggle for breath, to try to fight my way upward, but kind of indifferently, you know, like you do in a dream. I heard foggy faraway laughter. I seemed to be laughing myself. Then, abruptly, I lost consciousness.

I came back into it, or half-way into it, laying out on the prairie. My face was cleared of the strangling dirt. The foggy murmur of voices had taken on a different note—of argument. And another voice had been added.

. . . settle with Longie. . . . Hear me good. Aah, now, look. You look. Take a good look. This thirty-thirty is the last thing you're going to see if you don't start making tracks. . . .

I blanked out again.

I came back into full consciousness with a rush; lunged to my feet, looking wildly around me.

I was alone and little more than a hundred yards from the rear of my sleeping tent. Not far from the place where Four Trey and I had talked and shared whiskey only a few hours earlier. I could almost have believed that I had fallen asleep and had a nightmare. And I wished to God that I could have believed that, but it just wasn't in the cards.

There was my throbbing head for one thing; I hadn't gotten that from any dream. Then there was that voice I'd heard—

the voice of the man who had argued with the others and undoubtedly saved my life.

". . . *settle with Longie.*" He'd said that and a number of other things, things I'd forgotten, but which clearly indicated one thing. He'd known the people he argued with; not in the casual how-you-doin' way you knew most people in camp, but intimately. Almost the way he and I knew each other.

Because, of course, we did know each other. I had split a half-a-pint of whiskey with him that night and I had planned to tell him the terrible mess I was in with the Long gang. And he was a member of that gang.

But was *he* a member of the gang?

Couldn't it just be that he knew them, like he knew a lot of people, without actually being mixed up with them? He'd been knocking around in out-of-the-way places a long time before I bumped into him. He was a gambler, and when you gamble you look at a guy's money not the guy. He minded his own business and kept his mouth shut, so he got to know a lot of people who didn't ordinarily let themselves get known. And some of those people could have been the Longs.

That's the way it could have been. Whether it was or not I didn't know, and I didn't know how to find out.

I mean, how could you ask your best friend a thing like that? I figured the best way was to kind of ease into the question, come at it sort of sideways. But I didn't know how to begin. I was still trying to figure it out the next morning when we were back shooting powder together on the line. And I guess I must have been frowning pretty hard, looking like I was sore, because he spoke to me kind of apologetically.

"I'm afraid I haven't been very thoughtful, Tommy. I've kept you puzzling about some things that I should have explained to you."

"Well," I shrugged. "I, uh, figured you'd get around to it."

"I knew you were going to be cleared of killing Lassen because that girl, Carol, told me you would. She didn't say how, but she was so positive of it that I passed the word to you."

"I see," I said. "A pipeline hustler tells you that I'm going to be cleared, and. . . . Well, let it go. I guess the important thing is that I *was* cleared, not why."

He looked at me, then looked back at the dynamite he was capping and fusing. "Maybe she told you how she swung it. Or have you seen her since?"

I said she'd given me a pretty good idea of how she did it, the one time I'd seen her. "I've only seen her once, but I reckon you know that. You know I've never had a second chance to see her."

"It figures," he nodded casually. "A man doesn't go calling after he works mormon board and dope."

I said I wasn't working mormon board and dope now, so I guessed there wasn't anything to stop me from seeing her, was there? He spoke without looking at me, slowly tamping down the charge of dynamite.

"I'll check it back to you, Tommy. I certainly couldn't think of any reason that you can't. Now, let's fire this powder."

We fired it and scampered for cover. We came back to the ditch, and I started to pick up the conversation. But he shook his head firmly.

"Dyna's a jealous girl, Tommy. You give her all your attention or you wind up with half an ass."

"But we've got to talk!" I said. "You know we have to!"

"Mmm?" He cocked a brow at me. "Exactly what about?"

"Well, I, uh . . . I mean, I want to talk," I said. "You know, I think we ought to."

"So do I," he nodded. "But I think I can resist the temptation until lunchtime. Of course, if you don't feel that you can. . . ."

I said I thought I could probably make it. He said he was glad to hear it, and we went on with the job. I couldn't push him, you see. I didn't really have anything to push on and I guess I was probably afraid of finding out what I might. So I let it ride, and the morning passed. And then it was lunchtime.

We filled our trays along with one of the main work gangs, then carried them back up-line to where we would be alone. We began to eat, with me fumbling for words, trying to find the right kind of opening. I was still hunting for it when he gave me one himself.

"Do any writing in jail, Tommy? You know. . . ." He went on before I could answer him. "I think you ought to try a novel some time. Maybe a crime story. Take this pipeline, for example. Wouldn't it make a hell of a background for a payroll robbery?"

"It sure would," I said. "But I don't know where you'd

get your story. It's too simple, I mean. You just appear in camp with a dozen armed men—you've got them planted there ahead of time—and grab the loot."

"A dozen men against six hundred?" he shook his head. "You couldn't do it with six dozen. They'd scatter on you, spread all over hell and back, and you couldn't protect yourself against them. You'd get our brains beat out before you could say, Fire in the hole."

"But . . ." I hesitated, "I don't see that, Four Trey. You're armed and they're not. The money's insured. Why should they risk getting killed for dough that they'll eventually get, anyway?"

"Eventually? You mean in a month or two?" Four Trey grinned wryly. "You tell a pipeliner that he'll get his pay eventually and see what happens to you."

"But, dammit, I know damned well that . . . !" I broke off, swallowing the rest of the sentence. "All right," I said. "You don't wait until the money is in camp. You grab it before it gets there."

"How? Wait now. . . ." He held up a hand. "This is a true-to-life story, remember, so you can't twist your facts. You can't drag in an armored truck or have the money carried by a three-car caravan of deputy sheriffs."

"Of course not," I said. "They'd be hanging a bull's eye on themselves. The gang could just stake themselves out along the way, almost a hundred lonely miles in this case, and when the armored truck or whatever it was showed up, they'd knock it over. I don't claim that they wouldn't have some trouble, but. . . ."

"But it could be done," Four Trey nodded. "So you don't

use armored trucks or cop caravans in your story. On a job as far out as this one, the money would have to be brought in secretly in one of the company pick-ups or trucks. That's not positive protection against holdups, but it's the best that anyone's come up with."

I said, "Yeah, sure, I know. Pickups and trucks are going back and forth all the time. When they're not in use here, they're going into town or over to Matacora. They keep the road hot all day, hauling supplies and so on. So the money is concealed in one of 'em, and when it comes back. . . ."

"*Which* one is it concealed in? There are maybe twenty-five or thirty vehicles involved. How do you know which one is the money wagon?"

"Easy," I said. "The big boss is working with the gangsters. He tips 'em off."

Four Trey laughed. "Someone like Higby, you mean? He tips 'em off and points the finger right at himself?"

"Well . . . well, then, the driver tips 'em off!"

"Same deal. He'd be in the can before sundown, if the gang didn't kill him first. He'd have it coming to him, in my book, if he was stupid enough to expect any split but a split skull."

"But, uh. . . . Well, how about this? The company's field office is in Matacora; the bank is there. So the pickup or the flatbed would have to go all the way over to Matacora to get the payroll. Which means that it would have to get a darned early start out of camp to get back the same day. . . ."

"I'd say it would probably leave late the night before, wouldn't you? To play it absolutely safe, I mean. You can't have that much money on the road after dark, and it has to be here in plenty of time to pay the men."

"All right," I agreed, "it leaves the night before, which means that it'll be the first one back in camp. . . ."

"Oh, no, it doesn't mean that! What about all the company vehicles that are only running between here and town? They could get back a lot earlier than one coming all the way from Matacora."

"How about this?" I said. "The gang takes the license number of the truck or pickup when it leaves camp. . . ."

"Ah, Tommy," Four Trey sighed. "Tommy, my friend, don't you suppose the payroll insurers and the bankers and the pipeline big shots your gang is bucking would anticipate that? Don't you suppose they would take the very simple steps necessary to prevent identification by the license number or anything else?"

They would, of course. I hesitated a moment, then came up with a final idea: the gang would have a man posted in Matacora. When the money was picked up, he'd phone the town here and. . . .

"A question," Four Trey interrupted. "Just where in Matacora is your gang member going to be posted? At the bank or the company's field office? And what if the money driver didn't show up in either place? He wouldn't have to, you know. The money could be taken to him at some previously arranged meeting place. A hotel room, say."

The work whistle blew. Four Trey took a final swallow of coffee and emptied the rest onto the ground. He got to his feet, and I also stood up.

"Look," I said hoarsely. "Let's stop playing games. You've proved that the payroll can't be robbed; you tell me it can't in so many words. But I happen to know that. . . ."

"We're on company time, Tommy." He jerked his head up-line. "Let's start earning it."

"But I've got to know what's going on! Why tell me just enough to get me more mixed up than I already am?"

He sighed, hesitated. "Possibly because it's all I can tell you. I knew you were worried and I was trying to reassure you in the only way I could. But . . . that's all I can say. Now, let's get back to work."

"Is there going to be a robbery or not? What's going to happen when payday comes tomorrow?"

"You won't be here for it, Tommy. Not unless you get back on the job like I told you to."

He waited, staring at me evenly.

We went back to work.

We had to work overtime that night, and the chow flunky was late bringing grub to us. It was pretty sorry chow, too, by pipeline standards, and the flunky wasn't at all apologetic.

"You boes are lucky to be getting anything at all. You'll be getting a hell of a lot less tomorrow for breakfast and lunch."

"Says who?" I said.

"Says the man, that's who. We're jumping camp forty miles. How you goin' to fix chow when you're making a forty-mile jump?"

I looked from him to Four Trey. He didn't seem at all surprised.

"It makes sense," he murmured, pointing out that camp was more than twenty miles back of us now. "We can work both ways from the new camp and not have to jump so often."

181

"If it's so smart," I said, "why didn't we work both ways from the beginning?"

"Possibly because we have to learn from experience. Most of us do at least." He lighted a cigarette and passed the package to me. "Of course, you occasionally find a bright young man who knows all the answers in advance."

The chow flunky packed up and drove away. And I said I didn't pretend to know all the answers, but I'd sure like to know some.

"And I don't need any kidding," I said. "I need help. You know why I need it, and I've got no one to turn to but you."

"I am helping you. I have helped you."

"I know," I said. "I, uh, well, I was conscious part of the time last night, Four Trey. I . . ."

"Oh," he said softly. "I can see how that would throw you. Well, I thought you'd be better off not knowing certain things. But. . . ."

He wasn't a member of the gang, he said. He knew none of its members, although they all apparently knew him. As for the men who'd tried to kill me last night, well, it had been dark, and it was doubtful that he'd ever be able to identify them.

"But I do know Longie and his brothers, indirectly, through him. I've known Longden Long for almost ten years. We served time together. I'm responsible for bringing him and his gang here."

He pinched the fire from his cigarette, smashed it into the ground with his heel. Around us the silence deepened, the unearthly silence of prairie twilight. I gulped and my ears seemed to ring with the sound.

"*You,*" I said, at last. "You're a friend of that killer?"

"I didn't say that. Only that I'd known him for a long time. I saw this setup coming up here and I got word to him about it. He liked the looks of the deal, so he moved in with his gang."

"What about Higby? I figure you must have done a little fixing with him, too."

"Tommy . . ." He hesitated troubledly. "Forget Higby. I'm only putting the bug on my own back. I brought Longie and his gang here, but I wouldn't have done it if I'd known there was going to be a girl involved. In fact, I didn't know that he was taking me up on the deal until I spotted him in camp. I hadn't heard from him and I was kind of relieved that I hadn't, Tommy. I was glad—sort of—and then he showed up. And. . . ."

"But, *why?*" I said. "Why did you ever mix yourself up in such a mess in the first place? Why did you ever start it? You don't need the money. You could have made a baby fortune between here and the Gulf. Why . . . ?"

"How do you know what I need, Tommy?" He shook his head. "But never mind. I've told you as much as I can and probably more than I should. And now it's about time to go dance with Dyna."

He turned his hat brim up fore and back. Made motions of getting up. I said I didn't believe he was working with the Longs, even if they did think so.

"I know you too well, Four Trey. You're working for the law, aren't you? You and the sheriff and everyone are out to trap the Longs. Why, sure," I laughed, "that has to be it!

Every member of the gang will be out in the open for the first time, and. . . ."

"I'm working for myself, Tommy. Strictly."

"Oh, sure you are," I grinned, winking at him. "You'd have to say you were. You wouldn't dare admit the truth even to me."

"Particularly to you, Tommy—if it was the truth."

"What?" I said. "What's that supposed to mean?"

"Now, don't get your back up," he drawled. "You've got a lot going for you, my friend. You're smart and you've got guts and you're hell on wheels when it comes to dealing blackjack to a bunch of hardnoses. But I'd never let you play poker for me or chess. A couple of games, incidentally, which Longie Long is damned good at."

I looked down at the ground, my face reddening. I mumbled that I was sorry that he thought I was so stupid, and he sighed that he hadn't said anything of the kind.

"But you'd be bound to mix yourself up in this. With the best of intentions, of course, and the worst possible results. Certainly, you'd feel impelled to pass the word to your girl. Fortunately, or otherwise, I told you the truth in the beginning. I'm in this for myself for what it will do for me. Just me . . . no one else."

"Now, you wait a minute!" I jumped to my feet as he stood up. "What about my girl? What about Carol?"

"What about her? She'll be all right as long as she does what she's told."

"But. . . ."

"No more, Tommy." He turned away, drawing on his gloves. "Time to go back to work."

184

"Please," I said. "Just answer one question for me. Just one, and I won't ask you any more."

"All right, but make it fast."

"It's about tomorrow, payday. Will I be dealing blackjack for you?"

He hesitated; grinned at me crookedly. "A cute question, Tommy. But the answer is simple. You'll be dealing blackjack for me if there's a blackjack game."

Breakfast was doughnuts, coffee and dry cereal, with each man getting a can of evaporated milk. By ten in the morning, the chow and kitchen tents, the stoves, cooking utensils and so on were loaded onto flatbeds. They pulled out of camp for the new site with the cook and his staff riding the loads.

Four Trey and I blasted over the latrine and garbage pits. Then we turned to with the other men for the tearing down and loading. Everyone worked at it—machine men, welders, everyone—all six hundred men. Jumping a big camp was one hell of a big job, and every hand was needed. Also, the various jobs were interdependent, and when you pulled a bunch of men out of one place you soon halted work in another.

We had fruit, cookies and cold coffee for lunch. Afterwards, Higby assigned us a pickup and we packed and loaded our blasting materials.

Twenty cases of dynamite went into the back, each case wrapped in blankets and the whole load resting on bunk mattresses. I rode in the rear with it, kind of holding it down with my body. Four Trey drove, the supply of dynamite caps cradled in pillows on the seat beside him. And I guess you know we didn't take any passengers.

It was quite a ride, those forty miles. Not the kind I'd want to go through again. But it had one advantage; it sure took my mind off Carol and the Longs and all my other troubles. My mind was strictly on the load I was riding and those little black caps on the front seat, and I didn't have any trouble keeping it there.

There was no road after the end-of-line; not even the truck ruts that passed for a road. There were tracks across the prairie from the vehicles that had gone ahead of us, but they were so twisty and crisscrossed from the drivers trying to feel their way that they were virtually more harm than help.

We had to go very slowly, of course. The big flatbeds and pickups loaded with men and materials kept passing us. They swung wide around us, giving us plenty of room, then squared off to the south again and went jouncing and bouncing on their way until they faded into the rolling, sunbaked wilderness.

And it was a wilderness. In miles, we were no great distance from our former camp. But that had been the jumping-off place, you might say, the end of somewhere. And when you went beyond that, you were all-the-way gone.

Now and then a flatbed or pickup would pass us coming from the new camp, seeming to romp across the prairie as it burned daylight to make a final load. One truck from town passed us with booms and chains holding down its cargo of ice. The ice was melting fast, marking a trail toward the new camp. I might have wondered about it, why a tight-fisted outfit would pamper the men at such a busy time. But the only thing I was wondering about that day was how to stay alive.

Traveling so slowly, we didn't reach the new camp until almost four that afternoon, and it was nearly five by the time we had everything unloaded and stowed. We got busy with the other men then, wrapping up what remained of the work. Fortunately, there wasn't a lot of it, because the combination of scorching heat, back-breaking labor and short rations had just about wrapped *us* up.

Everyone was barely dragging tail; barely able to put one foot in front of the other. They lingered in the shade at every opportunity, sometimes flopping down flat on the ground.

It was more like a wake than payday. I sorted the Longs out of the crowd and saw that they were in no better shape than anyone else. Longden (Longie) Long passed me once and tried to muscle-up a grin, but he just didn't have it in him. A couple of times I took a long look at the tumbling terrain outside of camp, carefully searching the landscape for some sign of Carol or the housecar. There wasn't any. Neither in nor out of camp was there anything to indicate that a holdup was about to take place.

In fact, the way things stacked up, it was ridiculous to think that there might be a holdup.

It was almost six o'clock when Higby climbed up on the long wash bench and shouted that that was all she wrote. A few yells went up, pretty weak and weary ones, but enough to let him know that they were tickled to have it made. Someone shouted, "What about chow?" Not money but *food*.

Higby waved a pick handle, motioning everybody to come in close. As they did so, Depew climbed up on the wash bench with him, and a couple of timekeepers passed up a large cardboard box.

That would be the payroll box, I figured, loaded with the men's two weeks' earnings. That's what it was, too—and what it wasn't. But no one seemed much interested in it.

Depew whispered in Higby's ear. Higby frowned, then shrugged and nodded, banging the pick handle against the wash bench for attention.

"Now simmer down out there!" He stared sternly around the crowd. "Mr. Depew has something to say to you!"

Depew stepped forward, tried to glare around as Higby had. It got him a big laugh, which he didn't like at all. And when he opened his mouth and said, "Now, listen you men . . ." his voice came out in a high-pitched squeak.

A roar of laughter went up. He waited peevishly for it to die down, then started in again. "You men all know I'm your friend. . . ."

That was too much. Even Higby could hardly keep a straight face. You could have heard the laughter and jeering five miles away, and it got louder every time Depew tried to speak. He gave it up, finally; whirled around to leave. But he was so mad he couldn't see, I guess, because he fell smack off the bench. And what had happened before in the way of laughing wasn't anything to what happened then.

It was one great whooping and hollering, wave after mounting wave of it. A sound that went all the way through to your bones. Guys staggered around with tears in their eyes, doubling up and gasping for breath and finally getting so weak they had to sit down. Before the laughter had died, Higby began to speak.

The pipeline company was a big outfit. It had other jobs running besides this one, and some of those jobs were paid by check. So there'd been a little mixup. The company had sent checks here instead of cash. . . .

"Now, listen to me!" he shouted, raising his voice above the angry rumbling. "I've got some questions! How many of you want free cigarettes and cigars? Well, there's all you want over there," waving the pick handle toward the chow tent. "And that's not all that's there! How many of you want to stuff your guts with ice-cold potato salad—you heard me, *ice-cold*—and fried chicken and buttered rolls, the biggest by-God feast you ever saw in your life! Well, let me hear it!"

He heard it; cheers and yells of approval. But there was also an angry sullen rumbling. They were raging hungry, and the word *ice* was magic to them. But they wanted money, too. Not checks—where, for God's sake, could you cash a check? But *money*.

So they were pulled two ways. Teetering, they could swing one way as easily as another.

"How many of you want some free hours?" Higby was shouting again. "How many of you want to sack-in until nine tomorrow morning on company time? *How many of you want all the booze you can drink?*"

The anger, the grumbling sullen rumble wasn't quite gone. But it was weakening fast, all but lost in the cheering, shouting clamor for booze.

"Now, you're talking!" Higby grinned around at them. "By Christ, I almost believe you're pipeliners! So let's get it

189

wrapped up. Anyone that wants to can take his check and start walking. Right now! Because the rest of us are going to draw *cash-pay* for *four* weeks come next payday! The rest of us are going to have a party, *and we're starting right now!*"

He jumped down from the bench and headed for the chow tent.

For a split second longer, the mob continued to teeter, weighing disappointment against desire. Then, with a great happy roar they followed him.

Even the welders and machine men, who would as soon have had a check as cash, went along with the others.

Higby had done the impossible; what I would have thought impossible. Also, of course, either innocently or otherwise, he had arranged for the next payroll to be as large as the Longs had to have it.

The booze was a punch made of jake and fruit juice (and not much fruit juice). It hit a man fast and hard, and the camp was a howling riot inside of an hour.

Fights broke out everywhere. Except for a corps of high-pressure and strawbosses armed with pick handles, many men would have been killed. The high-pressure and straw-bosses had had drinks themselves—enough to put plenty of zip into their pick handles. When a guy got one of those hard-ash clubs against his head, the fight usually went out of him fast. *Usually*, it did. But not always.

There were a couple of guys, for example, who'd stolen butcher knives from the kitchen tent, and they were chasing around, claiming to be barbers and trying to give everyone shaves and haircuts. They practically got their ears knocked off with pick handles, and it just kind of acted like a tonic on 'em. The more they were clubbed the worse they got. So finally they had to be shot a little.

Just a little, you know. Not so bad that they couldn't be patched up in camp and go to work the next day. One of them had his little toe shot off and the other got a bullet through the palm of his hand. And they were pretty well-behaved after that.

A wild bunch of drunks was going around with a blanket, and tossing other guys in it. They were making a nutty game out of it, the idea being that they would all take a drink while the tossed guy was in the air. And they never did make it so far as I could see, but they acted like they had. Every time a guy would hit the ground, which was every time they did it, they'd all shake hands and congratulate each other, then start looking for another guy.

They were headed toward me, and I was waiting for them with a nice big tent stake, when the pick handle squad moved in and knocked 'em all senseless.

Some of the men had pipelined through the old Osage Indian Nation in Oklahoma, where they'd picked up the game of Indian ball. Even in those days the game had been outlawed for years, but these pipeliners had run across one somewhere, and they'd got a game going. Folks up in The Nation used to say that you didn't have to be a crazy drunk killer to play it, but it sure gave you a big edge.

The game didn't have any rules in the usual sense of the word. A ball was simply tossed into the air and two groups of people struggled for it. The groups could be of any size; and anything and everything went: kicking, gouging, biting, slugging. The game lasted until one side or the other was too bashed-up to continue.

Tonight a pillow was being used for a ball, and the playing field was the long wash bench. That added an extra hazard, what with men being thrown off and knocked off. So many men joined in the game, a couple of hundred of them it looked like, that the bench collapsed with their weight, and they all went down on the ground in a fighting howling tangle.

That didn't stop the game, of course. In fact, it made it worse. Clubs were ripped up out of the broken bench, and the players moved in on each other swinging. There were too many of them for the pick-handle boys to knock out and, of course, you couldn't shoot that many men even mildly. So the game went on, the bosses figuring, I suppose, that everyone was too drunk to get hurt very much.

I was standing back as far out of things as possible when Wingy Warfield sidled up to me. I'd made one big mistake, I guess, in calling him my pal and acting friendly, because he'd been latching onto me ever since, boasting and loud-mouthing and putting on airs.

"Well, Tommy," he said, wagging his head and trying to look important. "They can't say I didn't warn 'em. I told 'em, You give booze to a stinkin' bunch of jungle stiffs, an'. . . ."

"They're all right," I said coldly. "You're one of 'em, remember."

"Me?" He laughed like it was a joke. "No, sir, I don't have no part of that kind, Tommy. I've boomed from Ranger to Smackover t'Seminole, an' when it comes to that kind of trash. . . . Where you goin', Tommy?"

"To my bunk," I said.

"Want me to come in and set with you for a while? I can spare you a few minutes, I reckon. I mean, there ain't much I can do now, anyways, an' . . . Tommy?"

I kept on going without answering him.

My tent was empty, as I'd figured it would be. No one could have slept with the ruckus that was going on, and it just wouldn't have been smart to sack-in with so many drunks on the prowl. I sat down on the edge of my bunk and lighted a cigarette. I smoked it down and part of another, taking an occasional sip from my jake bowl. Giving Wingy plenty of time to lose himself.

I'd gotten a lousy headache; from the noise, I suppose, and fretting over things I couldn't help. It kept getting worse, and the jake began to do queasy things to my stomach. Finally, I jumped up and started back outside for some fresh air. And Bigger and Doss Long slid through the rear flap of the tent, and brother Longie came through the front.

They pinned me down pretty much as they had that day on the pipeline, Bigger and Doss sitting on either side of me on my bunk, and Longie hunkering down on the bunk in front of me. But there was one big difference between that day on the pipeline and now. Then we'd been out in the open—out in the daylight were everyone could see us and a shout would have brought help. Now, with six hundred men

193

around us, we couldn't have been more alone, and I could have yelled my lungs out without ever being heard.

"Now, Tommy, boy. . . ." Longie apparently saw how I felt and grinned reassuringly. "Just a friendly visit, Tommy. How you gettin' along, anyway?"

"I'm alive," I said, "no thanks to you. So maybe you'd just better mope off before I start thinkin' about it and get sore."

It was a pretty silly thing to say under the circumstances, and all three of them laughed. In their place, I'd've probably laughed, too.

"A real tiger, ain't he, boys?" Longie chuckled, and Doss and Bigger agreed that I was. "But this is friendly, Tommy. Pure friendly. We been out checkin' the countryside—gonna have us plenty of checkin' to do, y'know, after such a long jump—and we just thought we'd drop in for a chat. We figured you'd be lonesome, y'see, an'. . . ."

"Let's get it over with," I said. "What do you want to talk about? How smart you are? How you knew there was going to be a double payday right from the beginning?"

"Huh-uh. We want to talk about trouble, Tommy."

"Trouble?" I said.

"Trouble," Longie nodded. "You're a real smart young fella, Tommy boy. Oh, I know, I teased you a little, but pokin' fun is just a way of mine. I actually got plenty o' admiration for you, an' the boys here will tell you so."

"We sure will," Bigger said solemnly.

"It's God's truth," Doss declared. "Ol' Longie thinks you got a real head on you, Tommy boy, and Longie ain't never wrong about a man."

"Right!" Longie said. "Now, you talked pretty sharp

t'other night, Tommy; pointed out quite a few things that could go wrong on this little job we're plannin'. 'Course, it turned out that they *ain't* goin' to go wrong, they're not the problems you thought they was goin' to be. But just the same. . . . How do things look to you now, Tommy, boy?"

He was serious; they all were. They were convinced I knew something they hadn't foreseen. I hesitated, trying to think of a way to use the advantage, and Longie spoke again.

"How about it, Tommy, hmm? You tell us, an' I'll let you see Carol."

"Sure you will," I said. "Like you did the other night, huh?"

"I mean it, Tommy. We had her out ridin' with us, an' she ain't more'n a hundred yards from here, right now."

"Maybe," I said, my pulse suddenly pounding. "Maybe I go out to see her, and that's the last anyone sees of me."

"So don't go out," Longie shrugged. "We bring her in here. You just give us the straight dope, and we'll have her here in no more'n a minute!"

It was my turn to laugh. I said I didn't doubt his word of course—oh, no!—but I was getting kind of dizzy from all the hot air.

"You bring her in now," I said. "Just for a minute or two. I'll want to see her longer after I talk, but I'm sure going to see her for a minute or two *before* I talk."

They scowled, staring from one to the other. Bigger said that maybe Tommy-boy would talk without seein' her at all, but Longie curtly gestured him to silence.

"All right, Tommy. You got a deal. An' if you don't keep your end of it . . . !"

He jerked his head, and Doss arose and moved up to the

195

front flap of the tent. Bigger went out the rear, and he did not return. Or, at least, he did not come back inside. When the flap opened again, Carol came through it.

We had no chance to talk, with Longie standing by, and we couldn't have said anything, anyway, in the time we had. She was hardly in my arms, barely long enough for a quick kiss and a hug, before Longie was pulling her away and shoving her back out through the rear flap. Then, he and I and Doss sat down again, and I began to talk.

"Well, in the first place you made a big mistake in coming here at all," I said. "You don't know pipelines. You couldn't know what you were getting into until after you were in it. . . ."

I went on from there, building it up, repeating myself. Stalling while I dreamed up ways that the robbery would give them trouble. It wasn't to help them, of course. I guess you know what could happen to them, for all I cared. But if I could convince them that there shouldn't be a robbery, then they would have no need for Carol, and she and I. . . .

"Look, Tommy. . . ." Longie fidgeted impatiently. "We know all that. We know we can't get the money after it hits the camp, so we got to grab it on the way here. What. . . ."

"You can't get it on the way," I said, and I pointed out exactly why. "It looks easy to do, but when you. . . ."

"Goddammit!" Longie snarled. "Knock off the stalling! We made a bargain, and by God you ain't backin' out on it!"

"Who's trying to back out?" I said. "You asked me to tell you what I knew, and I'm telling you."

"Now, Tommy, boy. . . ." He made his voice amiable again. "Let me pin it down a little for you. We'd need a hundred men to take the dough after it reached camp. But takin' it on the way here; well, how many men do you need for that? A different story, ain't it? You shoot one man, the guy that's drivin' the money wagon, an' you're home free. So here's what I want to know, Tommy." He leaned forward on the bunk. "Why did Four Trey tell us the job would take every man we had?"

"Four Trey? What's he got to do with it?" I said.

"Ahh, come on, Tommy. You know his part in the picture. You'n him is best friends, an' he just naturally had to spill to you after he took you away from my boys. Now why did he tell us the job would take all our men when a blind idjit could see that it won't?"

"Well. . . ." I hesitated. "Maybe he didn't tell you everything. You see one way of pulling the robbery, he had another one in mind."

"Uh-*hah!*" Longie exclaimed. "Our way has some big holes in it, and not knowin' pipelines, we can't see 'em. But his. . . . Why you reckon he didn't tell us what his was, Tommy, boy?"

"To have an ace in the hole, why else? He's made it clear that you need all your men. What you don't know is why, and he can keep you walking damned straight until he tells you."

"Right, Tommy! Right! But he ain't told us an' he obviously ain't goin' to, so you just come clean like you promised. . . ."

"Look," I said uneasily. "I just made a guess, and you're taking it as fact. You've had plenty of chances to question Four Trey. Why didn't you do it?"

"Because we all of a sudden run out of chances a couple

of weeks before we figured to. There didn't seem to be no big hurry about it, and there wasn't no reason to think. . . . Yeah, Tommy, boy?"

"I don't know what the hell you're getting at," I said. "You seem to think Four Trey is pulling a double cross on you. If he is, he's got damned good reason to in my book. But that's not my problem. Iron it out with him, for God's sake! Go ask him your questions!"

"Ask *him*. Did you say to ask *him*, Tommy, boy?"

"What the hell do you think I said?"

Longie stared at me; exchanged a curious glance with Doss. "Now, Tommy, you can trust us. What have you got to lose, anyways?"

"Now, hear me!" I said. "Listen good! There's not a damned bit of use in coaxing or threatening me, because there's nothing I can tell you! I wouldn't tell you anything anyway if I thought it would help you, but. . . ."

"But you don't know," Longie said softly. "You don't know anything."

"He sure don't," Doss said. "Tommy Boy don't know from nothin'."

Longie squinted at me, thoughtfully; on the point, it seemed, of saying something else. Then, his eyes flickered, and his mouth twisted in a sudden grin.

"Well, what d'ya know," he drawled. "Right out in front of me, an' I didn't even see it."

He laughed, slapped me on the thigh and stood up. He jerked his head at Doss, and without another word they went out the back flap of the tent. I looked after them uneasily, wondering if I hadn't been a little out-of-line in talking to them about Four Trey. Offhand, I couldn't think of anything I'd said that might hurt him, but. . . .

Higby came in and gave me a curt nod as I stood up. There was a dried streak of blood at one corner of his mouth, and the pocket of his shirt was hanging by a thread. He sagged against the tent pole for a moment, then brought himself erect again.

"Putting you on powder in the morning, Burwell. Think you can handle it?"

"I've been doing it," I said.

"The head job, I mean. You're taking Four Trey's place."

"Take his place!" I said. "What . . . ?"

"Didn't know, huh?" He gave me a wryly shrewd glance. "He dragged-up a couple of hours ago. Rode out with the supply truck."

"B-But . . . why?" I said. "Why did he . . . ?"

"His business, Burwell. It's mine when they work; theirs when they quit."

The racket of the drunks roared suddenly to a deafening crescendo. Higby winced, his eyes squeezing shut for a moment, then turned savagely toward the entrance flap. "Pipeliners!"—it was like a cuss word, and yet there was something more. A kind of pride, maybe; a kind of affection; a double-tough father discussing his likewise children. "The ornery bastards! I wish every mother's son of 'em would die of the bleeding piles!"

He went out, gripping his pick handle like a ball bat.

I sagged down on my cot and buried my aching head in my hands. Baffled, wondering, the sickishness spreading from my stomach to my heart. I didn't know what to make of things. All that I could think of was that everything was getting to be too damned much! It had been too damned much from the moment I set foot in camp; hell, *even* before that!

I'd been slugged, I'd been jailed, I'd been fired. I'd almost been blown up, and jackhammered loose from my guts, and baked with pipe-dope and mormon-boarded to death. Everything that could be done to a man had been dished out to me from trying to bury me alive on down, and . . . and . . . !

And you showed 'em Tommy Burwell! You took it all and laughed at 'em and asked 'em where their men folks were. But enough is enough, by God! Enough is a plain big plenty! So if they try to hand you any more—just one more thing . . . !

"Heard about Four Trey, huh? Well, I could have warned you, Tommy." Wingy Warfield sat down in front of me, nodding his head wisely. "I been around since they spudded wells with rag line and a spring-pole, an' there ain't nothin' I couldn't tell you about Four Trey Whitey 'r anyone else. Why. . . ."

I raised my head from my hands and looked at him.

"Wingy," I said, "you better get long-gone from me."

"I know, I know how you feel, Tommy. You thought he was your friend, an' a fella's got to stick up for his friends. But I could tell you he wasn't no friend to no one! You know how I know? Well. . . ."

"Beat it," I said. "Wingy, if you don't get out of here . . . !"

"Well, I'll tell you, Tommy. I'll tell you God's truth. All the time you thought he was your friend, he . . . he, uh. . . . "

His voice trailed away as I stood up and lifted the end of

my cot. I began unscrewing the heavy leg, and he licked his lips nervously.

"Uh, Tommy, what was you studyin' to do?"

"You got a bray like a jackass," I said, "so I figure maybe you are one. An' the only way you can get through to a mule-jack is to hot his butt. You hot his butt real good with a club, an' he stops brayin' and starts listening. An' I'm going to have a first-rate hotting-club in just about a second!"

That second was about an hour longer than he needed.

He whipped out of there so fast that the breeze almost blew the lantern out.

So I became head powder monkey of the big line, maybe the last of the big lines, from furthest Far West Texas to Port Arthur on the Gulf. We were just bending the third week of the job, and I was the head shooter. Blasting a trail through a world where no man had gone before.

In the beginning, I worked in behind the jackhammers or we worked together. Then, we hit so much rock that it was better to have it cracked up a little for the hammers. So I moved out in front, cutting trail with rock-drill and Dyna and that cute black hat she wore, leading the long way to the Gulf.

Sometimes when the fire was in the hole, and I was taking distance from the blast, I'd look back down the line behind me. And it seemed like as long as I looked I could never look enough. There was so much to see, so much that would never be seen again. *Pasó por aquí*—passed by here. And then no more.

Men and machines, stretching endlessly into the distance. Men and machines, only a thin almost invisible rivulet at first, a tiny thing lost in the horizon. It seemed to come up out of the ground like a puny spring, back there at the start; a near-nothingness amidst nothing. And then slowly it grew larger, the men and machines grew larger, and the sound of them grew greater; the rivulet became a river, and its thunderous surging shook the earth.

The long thin line of burnt-black men, their shovels glinting as they caught the sun . . .

The yellow-painted generators, peering down into the ditch, periodically breaking into fits of chugging and coughing as though startled by their surroundings. . . .

The mammoth ditchers rocking to and fro, grunting and quavering like fat old ladies. . . .

The jackhammers jouncing and jigging as they pounded the hard rock. . . .

The razzle-dazzle of sparks raining upward where welders' torches pencilled fire against the pipe . . .

> *Throw out the lifeline,*
> *Here comes the pipeline.*
> *Somebody's going to drag up!*

A lot of 'em would drag up, I reckoned. Paid off with money or the ditch for a grave. *Pasó por aquí*—and then no more.

But it was something to see, something to remember. The men and the machines—dying, smashing up, wearing out—but always moving forward. Creeping through a wild and lonely world toward Port Arthur on the Gulf.

I kid you not when I tell you the powder still scared hell out of me. My grandparents, the only parents I'd ever known, had gone to heaven in little pieces, and a thing like that you never get over. But being scared doesn't need to paralyze a man, unless he lets it. Being scared is about the best way I know of being healthy.

Dyna was a touchy girl, but she was absolutely predictable. You knew how she had to be treated, and as long as you treated her exactly that way you got along fine. But never slight her, or it'd be the last time you did. Never let your mind wander when she demanded your attention.

Dyna was a good girl, but jealous, and any two-timing would get you killed. So I was scared of her and glad that I was. We got along, Dyna and I did, despite me having the world's dumbest helper.

He was always making talk instead of keeping his mind on his job. Sometimes, it looked like, he didn't have any mind to keep on it. A hundred times I told him how to tamp his shots down, and he'd do it the same damned way every time. Like he was tickling rattlesnakes with a short feather. Then, when the shots got buried, he'd hang back and wait for me to dig 'em out.

Finally, he buried Dyna for the second time in a morning, and that was just one time too many. So while he was hanging back and sort of scuffling his feet and mumbling that he was sorry, I picked up a rock drill and motioned him over to me.

"You got a choice," I said. "You can either dig this drill out of your tail or you can dig those shots out of the ground."

He told me I could screw it; he'd set in on another job or drag-up. I told him he could go suck hind titty from a tumblebug, but not until he got those shots out. So we had a few more words, and I had to bust him a couple of times, but then he saw it my way.

I was sitting back out of range while he uncovered the shots when Higby drove up and asked me what the trouble was. I explained that there wasn't any trouble; I was just trying to teach the guy a lesson. Higby said he guessed it was the only way.

"Want to get rid of him, Tommy? Say the word, and I'll give you another helper."

"Aw, naw, he'll make it all right," I said. "He's not a bad kid as kids go these days."

"Kid? Kids must have grown a lot older since the last time I looked."

"That's it exactly," I said. "They get older but they don't get any smarter. Why, I'll tell you, Mr. Higby. . . ."

I broke off because he'd all of a sudden got a bad fit of coughing and had to turn his head. After a moment or two, he turned back around, his face red from coughing.

"Uh, yes, Tommy? You were saying?"

"I was saying I don't know what's going to become of the world," I said. "But, by God, I fear for it, with this new generation of kids that's coming along! Now, back in my day. . . ."

Higby started coughing again. He drove away coughing, waving me so-long over his shoulder instead of saying it.

I'd decided I liked Higby. I still didn't know whether he was a crook or not, but I knew he was a man and I liked him.

Somehow, I found out that I didn't know a lot about a lot of things I'd once known all about. Not so long ago, I'd felt that I had to know everything about everything and I was afraid to admit that I didn't. But now it didn't seem to matter. Being ignorant isn't the same as being stupid, and I knew I could learn when it was time to.

There was all the difference in the world between being head powder monkey and an assistant. The difference of responsibility. Time and money and life itself was being bet on me, on the belief that I would blow clean ditch with no costly delays and without endangering lives. Living up to that responsibility kept my days so crowded that they seemed more like weeks than days, even though they rushed by. Living up to responsibility gave me confidence that I had never had before.

I *knew* that I was worthwhile. Knowing it, I no longer had to try to keep proving it.

Sometimes, riding into camp at night, I would stand up on the jolting flatbed and look off across the prairie to where Carol was or where I thought she would be; occasionally, if I had gauged things correctly, getting a glimpse of her and her camp down in a little hollow as it had been before. I would stand there in the late afternoon sunlight, rocking and swaying with the truck, my hat brim cocked up front and back and my bare torso gleaming brown through the gray powder of rock dust, and over the rolling expanse of sage and short-grass, I would send her a message. Telling her to sit tight and take it easy. Telling her that I would work things out some way, and there wasn't a thing for her to worry about.

I knew that I *would* work them out, too. She was my responsibility, so I'd do it.

No, I didn't know how. *How* was jumping the gun, and before I could get to it I had to know something else. At one time—only a short time before—I wouldn't have bothered with it. But now, at last, I was thinking, looking at a problem from all sides before I jumped in and tried to solve it. Now I was being responsible. So I knew I had to know the *why* of things or I'd never live to get to the *how*.

There was no way that I could see that the Long gang could pull their robbery. Rightly or wrongly, however, Longie believed that there was a way. But *if* there was, he himself had practically admitted that it would require no more than one or two of his men.

It seemed to me that he should have been glad of this. The fewer men required the easier the job. But he wasn't glad. He was alarmed. *Why?*

Longie seemed virtually convinced that Four Trey had deliberately misled him into bringing his entire gang for the robbery instead of the one or two that were needed. *Why?* What could Four Trey have gained by such a deception?

To move back a little bit, what had been Four Trey's motive in acting as fingerman for the gang? *Why* had he wanted the robbery? Any cut he could get from it would be far less than he would make by working and gambling. So, *why . . . why,* when he never needed money . . . ?

Well, you see? The answer to one question was the answer to several.

If Four Trey's motive wasn't money, as it obviously wasn't, then it could only be one other thing. Revenge. That accounted for Longie's suspicions, his alarm. Four Trey had gotten the whole gang here, because he meant to take revenge against them all. He had no faith in Texas justice, with the pardon-selling Parkers in power, so—

But wait a minute! Why did Four Trey have a grudge against everyone in the gang? *How could he have when he didn't know who they were?* And, of course, he didn't. No one did, outside the gang itself. He would know who they were when they all came together for the robbery or their getaway, but until then . . . And how would that change anything? To have a grudge against them, all of them, he would have had to know them beforehand. So, why, since that wasn't possible . . . ?

Night after night, I lay in my bunk and puzzled over the riddle. Probing its contradictory parts until I was worn out and fell asleep. Repeatedly coming up with an answer that was no answer.

Four Trey hadn't been willing to let the law settle with the gang. He'd meant to do it himself, and there was only one way he could do that.

By killing them! Killing a minimum of a dozen men, practically all of them strangers to him!

It didn't make sense . . . did it? Or if there was logic to it, if he did hate them that much, then why had he suddenly abandoned the plan—as he had had to in dragging-up and leaving camp?

Or had he had to? Wasn't that merely a necessary part of the plan?

The Longs had wanted to know why he'd brought them all here for a job when no more than two would be needed. He couldn't tell them why, so he'd had to leave, and—

And . . . ?

I didn't know, but I knew I was coming close to knowing. The *why* of his grudge. The *why* of his killing men he didn't know. The *why* of his apparent dropping of a plan he had been determined to carry out.

I was thinking, *really* thinking, for the first time in my life, and I could feel myself drawing closer to the answer. And finally I reached it—almost.

It was during my second week as head-shooter. I'd come in from work too dirty and sweaty for ordinary washing, so after supper I walked down to the Pecos for a bath. The river roughly paralleled the line for much of its distance, and it was only about a mile away at this point. I worked my way through the scrub-growth along the bank, then paused at its edge to look down into the stream bed.

In this season, the Pecos was more a series of pools than a river; ponds of various sizes, with only a narrow film of water running over the stretches of gravel and sand between them. Now, in the cool shade of evening, animals and birds were clustered around the pools, coming and going from them in a peaceful and orderly procession.

I saw a wolf, two coyotes, three of the big woodcats who considered the river their own happy home; more rabbits and quail and pheasant then I could count. Sometimes there was just a little teeth-snapping when a bathing bird wing-splashed water on a drinking animal. But it was just a warning, nothing more. This was the end of the day, and everyone had fought and fed enough, and now was the time of truce. Up and down river, as far as I could see, they stood drinking side by side— the natural enemies, so-called—and I watched and kind of wondered if there were any natural enemies, or whether there was ever any enemy anywhere but hunger.

I hated to disturb them, but I couldn't stay there indefinitely, so I went on down the bank and began to bathe in the nearest pool. Some of the birds made a fuss about it, screeching and batting at me with their wings. The animals moved leisurely away to another watering place. Hardly looking at me after the first deceptively lazy glance, apparently sizing me up as a party to the general truce.

I still reckon it as the nicest compliment I've ever had.

When I had washed good, I sauntered naked up the sandy shore, letting the sun dry my body. It was nice to walk there, with all the life around me and none of it afraid, and I went further than I intended to. So at last, I saw it—something up against the shelving bank of the river. I hunkered down in front of it, my pulse beginning to pound with excitement.

Gray ashes. The remnants of a tiny fire. A recent one apparently, since the ashes were unlumped with dew. I sifted them through my hand and came up with something else. A tiny shred of wood shaving. And probing through the surrounding bushes, I found what it had come from.

A piece of board, the kind that boxes are made of. Just what kind I couldn't say, since it had been pretty well shaved for fire.

I sniffed it, and I still wasn't sure. There was a very faint odor of dynamite, but it was likely that it came from me.

I put the piece of wood back in the bushes and glanced around casually. Pecos River water was drinkable if you didn't mind a few wiggle-tails. As for food, well, there was all that a man could want for the taking. He could live here forever, and as long as he kept his fire small and his eyes open, no one would know it.

I went back downstream to where I'd left my clothes. I dressed slowly, wondering what my next step should be, finally deciding that there was no next step to be taken here.

He didn't want to be found. That being the case, it wasn't likely that I could find him even if I tried, and there would have been no point to it, anyway. He was too determined. He wouldn't have gone to these lengths if he hadn't been dead-set on going ahead.

Yet—I went back up the river bank and headed for camp— yet it wasn't like him to do what he apparently intended to do. He just didn't care enough, you know? He wouldn't let himself care. And when a man's like that, when he just doesn't give a damn, how can he get sore enough to kill?

Of course, he hadn't always been that way. He'd cared so much—possibly too much—for his wife that when he lost her . . .

I stopped dead in my tracks. *Lost her how?*

He hadn't said, but suddenly I knew. I was almost positive. To make absolutely sure I would have to talk to someone— but not yet. Not until the very last, the night before payday. Not until it was too late for him to talk.

Meanwhile, there were other things to be done.

210

I was wearing my shirt when I rode in from work the next night. I kept it buttoned good and my shirttails tucked in tight, and I was plenty careful how I moved around.

Instead of heading right for the wash bench when I got in, I made like I was going to the latrine, then hustled on out of camp until I reached a certain clump of bushes. I got rid of what I was carrying there, caching it so it couldn't be seen. The next night I brought in another load, and another one the third night. You'll understand that they couldn't be very big loads—not loads at all, in the ordinary sense. But I figured that the three loads would be enough for the job I had to do . . . *if* I had one to do. If I just wasn't acting nutty like Four Trey had hinted I did.

I reckoned a gun might have been better, handier and safer and all. But there was just no way I could come by one, and I needed a weapon, so I used what I had.

I had a couple of cigars and a supply of tying twine in the cache. Also two eight-once bottles of jake that I'd coaxed out of the cook.

That was it, then.

And, then, it was the night before payday.

I sidled up to Wingy Warfield as he was setting out basins on the wash bench. He scowled at me, starting to tell me off with his jackass bray, but I shut him up with a five-spot and began talking fast.

"I sure owe you an apology," I said. "I shouldn't ever have believed Four Trey when he said you'd been dirty-naming me all over camp. That's why I was sore, see, an'. . . ."

"Why, the dirty—! That just ain't so, Tommy! I—"

"Sssh, not so loud!" I said. "I know it isn't so, Wingy. He just did it to make trouble between us, because that's the kind of a guy he is. Now I know you don't like to talk about people—it just isn't your way. But I figure you know plenty of dirt about him—"

"Damned right, I do! Why, I been on the boom since—"

"Sure, sure," I said. "So if you could give me the word, I'd spread it around with everyone, and . . . not here! He's a dangerous man, and he's probably still got friends in camp. And if they saw us talking together . . ."

"Uh, yeah." He wet his lips uneasily. "Maybe we better make it outside of camp, huh? After dark."

"I know just the place," I said.

He hunkered down near me behind the clump of bushes. Jerking his head to an offer of a drink. His voice shaky with fear.

"Uh, I been thinkin', Tommy. Me'n Four Trey has always been good friends, an' I, uh, reckon I don't really know no dirt about him. I sure wouldn't want to say anything that would hurt his feelin's or, uh, make him sore at me, so—"

"Sure," I said. "I kind of feel the same way, Wingy. Why don't we just have a drink and forget it?"

"I don't drink, Tommy. You know that. I sure wouldn't drink no jake if I did."

I said I sure wouldn't either. I'd never done it in my life and I was too old to start in. Wingy frowned puzzledly, staring at the bottle in my hand.

"Ain't that what you're drinkin'?"

"Of course not," I said. "It's one hundred per cent pure Jamaica ginger like it says on the label. See? It's right there in plain sight."

"Uh, yeah, but—"

"It's not jake until you foul it up with juice like the jungle-bums do. Catch me doing a thing like that! No, siree! I just follow the doctor's advice, and mix it with pure water. Like this, see? That makes it into a medicine, what they call an antiseptic. It kills the deadly germs a guy picks up from handling dirty washbasins and so on."

He glanced uneasily at his hands; scrubbed them nervously against his pants. I said I'd probably be dead right now of syph or clap if it wasn't for dosing myself with good old 100 per cent pure Jamaica ginger like the doctors had advised me to.

"There's an awful lot of dirty diseases going around a big camp, you know. And the guys that have 'em are always the ones that make messes for other people to clean up. They'll filthy up a wash bench or a basin, and leave it for some poor devil to—uh—well, never mind," I said. "What kind of germ-killer do you use, Wingy?"

"I, uh, I sort of disremember," Wingy said. "You mind fixin' me a drink of that 100 per cent pure Jamaica ginger?"

He didn't have anything useful to say at first. Just lies, mostly, about how Four Trey cheated at dice and dirty-named people who'd never spoken anything but good of him. Then, when he was near the end of his second bowl of jake and water, he mentioned that Four Trey had been in the pen. I said I'd heard that, but I'd never found out why.

"Well, I'll just tell you, then!" Wingy took a big slurp of his drink. "Damn, that's good germ-killer! Best I ever used— *hic!* An' here's why Four Trey got sent up. Leastwise, it's why folks *say* he was sent up. I wouldn't want you to say I said so, because all I'm sayin' is what was said t'me, an' that's not the same as if I was sayin' I said, uh— Le's see, le's jus' see. Oh, yeah. He served time for breakin' and enterin'. That's it! Breakin' and enterin'."

"Aw, come on, Wingy." I laughed, pretending not to believe him. "Four Trey's too smart to do anything like that. He sure as hell wouldn't get himself caught if he did."

"An' what if he was drunk, huh? What if he'd been drinkin' s'long it was runnin' out of his ears, an' his brains along with it? What if—*hic, hup!* Gimme another drink of that 100 per cent pure Germaica killer!"

I mixed it very slowly, still pretending not to believe him. Wingy said it was so, *irregardless,* because he'd got it straight from a guy who knew a guy who had a second cousin livin' in Four Trey's hometown.

"It was on account of his wife, see? He went haywire after

214

his wife got killed an' he finally wound up breakin' and enterin', like I told you!"

"Lay off," I laughed. "Now, you're getting worse and worse. There's not a woman in the world who could throw Four Trey Whiteside!"

Wingy took the drink from my hands; swallowed a sulky sip of it. He didn't say anything for a minute or two, and I was afraid I might have pushed him too far. But then he belched, the jake fumes tickling his nose, and he laughed good-naturedly.

"Is kind of stupid, ain't it? But, anyways, that's the story. Four Trey an' her, they'd knowed each other since they was kids, wasn't much more'n kids when they got married, an when she got killed—*hic!*—well. . . ."

"Y'know, it just might be true," I said. "It's just wild enough to be true. What was her name, anyway?"

"What's the difference? How'n hell's anyone gonna know stupid thing like that?"

"Well, I just supposed it was in the papers—it usually is when someone gets killed—and—"

"Huh-uh! Aw, no, it ain't! Not unless it's someone important. Because no one gives a damn, right? You 'r me 'r poor li'l girl gets killed n-nobody ca-ca-cares. Jus' throw us all inna ditch, you n' me' poor li'l girl an'—an'—"

He began to cry. I patted him on the back and comforted him, and after a stiff drink he got squared away again.

Four Trey's wife, he said (just sayin' what had been said to him) had worked in a factory or a bank, "or somethin' like that." It had been held up, and there had been a hell of a big commotion, and when the smoke cleared away and the holdup gang had cleared out, she was dead. Yessir, that poor li'l girl was shot deader'n dead. An' then Four Trey had started goin' to pieces, an' a year or so later he'd got sent up for breakin' and enterin'.

"Pretty rich, ain't it?" Wingy glared angrily into his drink. "They can't catch the fellas that killed his wife—least they never tried no one for it. But they grab him right off f'r breakin' into a guy's house when he was too drunk to know better!"

"Hmm," I said thoughtfully. "I wonder if he ever found out who did it? I mean, he might have been in prison at the same time some of the holdup guys were, and they might have peeped to him without knowin' who he was."

"Wha' ya mean they wouldn't know?" The jake was making Wingy cross. "Knew his name, didn't they?"

"But they didn't know *hers*. It hadn't gotten any publicity, and there'd never been a trial or—"

"G'dammit, wouldn't have made no difference, nohow! Couldn't find out somethin' that nobody knows, could he? Lotsa shootin' goin' on. Big gang o' guys an' all shootin'. S-s-soo—*hic!*—couldn' say which one did it. On'y way t' make sure of gettin' the guy'd be to get 'em all. . . ."

The last sentence was the clincher for me. It took the babbling, drunken meanderings, the gossip of the camp loudmouth—a guy who would climb a tree to lie when he could stand on the ground and be truthful—to tie them into fact.

On'y way t' make sure of gettin' the guy'd be to get 'em all. . . .

Which was just what Four Trey intended to do.

I had been reasonably sure of it before talking to Wingy. I—a guy on the outside had seen it—and if I had then Longie had. And Four Trey must have figured that he would. So why he was going ahead anyway, one man tying into a dozen— all of them armed and waiting for him—

There was no time for puzzling out the riddle. All hell was about to pop, and Carol and Four Trey would be caught right in the big middle of it. And all I could do was be on hand to help them.

Back in camp, the motor of a flatbed roared to life, then the engine of a pickup. They pulled out of camp together, both ostensibly heading for the long run to Matacora. Either one could return with the payroll money, and the gang had no way of knowing which. But I reckoned that that wouldn't make any problem for Longie Long. He'd know just what to do about it.

Wingy mumbled, "Gimme 'nother drink o' that... 'at..." Then he laughed, tossed his bowl in the air with a "Whoopie!" and went over backwards.

I caught him, eased him down to the ground and pulled his jumper around his shoulders. He began to snore deeply, dead to the world.

I left him there, feeling a little guilty about it, although there was no reason why I should have. He was a boomer, the longest-time boomer around. He'd boomed through every field from Wyoming to West Virginia, from Sweetwater to Seminole. He'd done more sleeping on the ground than he had in bed and he'd been bitten and chewed on by everything that walked or crawled. And I doubted that anything could hurt him short of a two-legged animal with a gun.

The night wasn't dark, and it wasn't light. It was one of those middling nights, the kind where you can see something if you're straining to. If you know what you're looking for and where to look for it. So, careful as the guy was, I saw him.

He was crawling under the row of flatbeds and pickups. Remaining only a minute or so under each one, then moving on to the next one. I don't know what he could do to them in so short a time, but you could bet he knew exactly what he was doing. Whatever was necessary to knock them out of commission. Cars and trucks were put together a lot simpler in those days, and it was easy to get to a vital spot in their innards.

He crawled out from under the rear of the last vehicle—a flatbed—and kept on crawling until he was well out on the prairie. Then, he stood up and sauntered away in the darkness.

The rest of the gang had already gone ahead of him. He had had to stay behind, unable to do his job until the flatbed and pickup had pulled out for Matacora. And now he was gone to join the others.

I stood up, on the point of trailing him, then decided that the risk wasn't necessary. The gang would collect at the place where Carol had been camping. They would want to be sure that Four Trey would find them, and that was the only way they could be sure.

I went around the end of camp and headed across the prairie. Straight toward the place where the gang and Carol would be—and maybe Four Trey, by this time. And, then, again I had a change of mind. Because they'd probably be anticipating trouble from camp. If trouble was going to come, it would have to come from there, so they'd be watching for it. Quite likely, they'd be looking for me to blunder in on them, because I sure hadn't been very smart in the past.

Well, anyway, I thought it over for a minute or two. Then, in place of going straight ahead, I angled off, moving south and a little east and slowly coming around in a wide arc. I couldn't exactly pinpoint the spot where they were, but I knew it was roughly east of camp and a little over a mile from it. So, by using the camp lights as a guide, it was no great problem to keep my bearings.

The problem was moving. Fast enough, I mean.

I was wearing a little tying-twine harness around my chest, up where I could watch it and get at it. There were six sticks of dynamite in it, all capped, of course, and with fuses as short as I could cut.

With a load like that tied onto you, you don't hurry so good. Not over rough ground in the dark. With a load like that, the first time you stumble will be the last time, and you'll travel a lot further and faster than you counted on.

So I had to take it very easy, and I had to take a long detour to where I was going. I was short on time—maybe a lot shorter than I thought. But it was that or nothing, and that's no choice.

I reached the end of the arc, the point where I would cut sharply to the west. I stooped down low behind a thick growth of sage and struck a match to my cigar. Lighting it so fast that there was the merest flicker of light. On and gone before anyone could be sure he had seen it.

I took a deep puff or two, shielding the glow with my hands. I let the ash grow over the coal, protecting and hiding it. Then, I was ready for the backstretch. Or as ready as I'd ever be.

If the gang was only guarding the other side, I had a chance—and Carol and Four Trey had one. But if they had someone on this side, the rear approach . . .

And they did.

It was lucky that I was forced to move so carefully, kind of making a chore out of it each time I lifted a foot and set it down in front of the other one. Otherwise I might not have heard it. The soft *chuff-chuff* of a spade.

I crept forward, guided by the sound. Getting in fairly close before I finally saw him. I was moving in still closer when he stabbed the spade into the ground with a sharp *chuff*, leaving it standing upright as he stooped.

He laughed, a mean, teasing laugh. Then his jeering voice drifted to me, speaking to someone on the ground.

"*. . . sorry, honey, but you just hadn't ought to've knowed . . . little Mexico job we pulled. Them spics . . . ever . . . we done it . . . wouldn't like us a-tall . . .*"

There was a frantic, smothered sound. Terrified, choked. Suddenly I knew what it was, what was going on.

Carol. Carol, bound and gagged and about to be buried alive.

He laughed again, spoke to her with mock sympathy. He was goin' to tuck her in real nice, he said. Real nice an' cozy. Might be a mite lonesome at first, but pretty soon all sorts of things would be cuddlin' up to her. Fire ants an' tumble-bugs, an' snakes an'—

A real funny guy, you know? He was laughing and having so much fun that I was right on top of him before he knew it. Which was just about the last thing he ever knew.

I swung with my razor-sharp shooter's knife, just one sweeping slash across his throat. He sagged backwards on his heels, knees buckling, and toppled into the grave he'd dug for her. And that was the end of his laughing and teasing. The end of him.

I spoke to Carol, whispered to her, rather. Letting her know who I was, warning her not to cry out. Then, I got her un-gagged and cut her bonds. And then, well, I sort of held her for a minute, and she sort of held me. And she cried a little bit, but just out of happiness and relief. So softly that it couldn't have been heard.

They had Four Trey, she told me. They'd caught him as he was approaching them. He wasn't armed—apparently he'd ditched whatever weapons he had when he saw he was going to be caught. But his story (which they didn't believe, of course) was that he hadn't been carrying any.

"That's right, Tommy," Carol whispered. "He said he'd been meaning to kill them all, but he'd changed his mind. He'd settle for having them give themselves up."

He'd settle for it? *He* would? I reckoned they'd got a big laugh out of that.

"Why haven't they killed him?" I whispered.

"They're going to, as soon as Longie's through with him. Longie jokes a lot, and he says there's plenty of time."

We whispered together a little longer. Then, I told her to swing wide, like I had, and head for the pipeline camp. She didn't want to (and, as it turned out, she didn't). She wanted to stay and try to help. But I got kind of tough about it, so finally she started away in the darkness, and I moved forward again.

I came up on a little rise to see a faint glow ahead of me. The dimmed light of a lantern which seemed to rise up out of the earth. That would be where the car was parked, the low dip in the prairie. Where the gang and Four Trey were. A few yards further along and I could hear them; Longie's drawled questions and the whoops of laughter as Four Trey answered them.

I paused, running my hands over the dynamite harness, making sure the sticks were all riding good. I cupped my hands around my cigar, and drew the coal alive with a long puff.

The gang's laughter tapered off into silence. An ominous note came into Longie's amused drawl.

And then suddenly I was there, as close as I could get to them. Not fifty feet away and looking down on them from above.

Longie was sitting in the tail-end of the housecar, his legs dangling over the side. Four Trey was standing a few feet in front of him, and the others were kind of ringed around him in a half-circle. They were all crowded together, which made my dynamite about as useless as so many sticks of candy. I hesitated, wondering what I'd better do, as Longie spoke again.

"You think I didn't see through it, Four Trey? You think I didn't know it was all a setup right from the beginnin'? Why, hell, I almost laughed in their faces! A Square John goin' crooked just when a smart sheriff turns stupid! A damn fool would've knowed it was a trap, an' I ain't no fool!"

"You're not, huh?" Four Trey made a pretense of yawning. "You figure it's smart to walk into a trap with your eyes open?"

Longie said he sure as hell did, because it wasn't a trap no more when a man had his eyes open. The law had been tryin' to trap him and his boys for years, and they'd walked off with the bait every time.

"Only one thing I didn't know, Four Trey. I wasn't sure of it, anyways. That was where you fitted into the picture. But when you skipped out, and when I got to thinking back on all those questions you used to ask when we were doin' time together. . . ."

"Forget it!" Four Trey cut in on him. "You're smart and everyone else is stupid. But it still doesn't change anything. I've tipped off the sheriff, and there won't be any payroll coming through."

Longie laughed angrily. "Now, I reckon that's not so, ol' friend Four Trey. What you told the sheriff was that we wasn't goin' to rob the payroll this time. You told him there'd been some kind of hitch, car trouble prob'ly, and we'd have to wait for the next time around. That's what happened, and don't tell me it ain't neither. Because you figured to kill us yourself and you didn't want no law buttin' in!"

Four Trey hesitated; nodded. "All right. I changed my mind, but that is what I'd planned. But there still won't. . . ."

"Don't you say it, you lyin' son-of-a-bitch! They can't stall the men another payday, an' the sheriff don't see no reason to stall. So the money'll be comin' through all right. An' it'll be on one of the only two things that's left runnin'. All we got to do is knock out the only truck and the only pickup that comes down the trail, and we've got the score made!"

"You'll never swing it." Four Trey didn't sound very convincing. "Pipeline traffic is about all there is out here. What do you think will happen when it's chopped down to two vehicles?"

"Some tall wonderin', I reckon. But they'll be practically here by then. So. . . ." Longie slid down to the ground. "So that'll be the end of their wonderin', and them, too. An' speakin' of ending things. . . ."

He jerked his head, gesturing. The gang began to close in on Four Trey, and then. . . .

A fist slammed into the back of my neck. I stumbled and went down, and there was a triumphant yell from Doss.

"Got him, *Longie! I got the punk!"*

The stumble helped; kept me from falling flat on my chest. Instinctively, I thrust out my elbows, catching some of my weight on them, and that helped, too. So I didn't slam down on the ground like I might have. I went down hard, but with just a little less impact than dyna takes to explode. And that little was as good as plenty. Like I say, dyna's a good girl as long as you don't crowd her. Which, apparently, was just what that damned Doss was determined to do. He was trying to grind me into the ground at any rate, which worked out to the same thing.

He'd come up on me from behind, so he didn't know I was a walking bomb. He hadn't seen the dyna, and I couldn't tell him about it, because he had his knees in my back and my mouth and nose crushed into the earth. I struggled, tried to yell. He bore down all the harder, and I strangled and began to lose consciousness.

And there was a burning in my chest. And the smell of smoke. And, vaguely, I wondered where my cigar was.

The weight suddenly went off of me. Doss yanked me to my feet, gave me a shove down the slope. I was dazed, wobbly. So, after a step or two, he grabbed my arm and started to hustle me along with him.

"Punk son-of-a-bitch! I'll . . . I'll. . . ."

He saw it then, the charred ring of fire on my shirt. The sputtering fuses of the dynamite. The others had been staring up at us and now they saw it, too. And he and the others, all seemed to yell, to move at the same time.

One moment they stood frozen, speechless. The next, they were yelling, scrambling to get the hell away from me.

"Yeow . . . !"

"Gangway! How the hell . . . !"

"Where's Bobo? Where . . . ?"

"The car, the car, the car . . . !"

There was the *craack-craack* of a rifle, and the lantern

shattered and went out. Car doors slammed, and the starter whirred. I came alive suddenly, began clawing at the dyna.

I hit the rear of the car with the first stick. A pure lucky hit because I wasn't taking aim, just trying to get it away from me. The car rocked forward, its windows shattering. The scorched air of the backblast slapped me in the face, and my eyes filled with pale smoke. But I grabbed loose two more sticks and threw them, one with each hand. As they exploded in the air, the car roared and rolled away.

I didn't have time to throw the last three sticks. The fuses were almost burned into the caps, and I knew I'd never make it. And I didn't have to, either.

Four Trey grabbed me. He yanked the whole harness loose with a jerk. Threw it with one hand as he bore me down to the ground with the other. I slapped my hands over my ears, just as all three sticks went off together. But I was almost stone deaf for the next couple minutes.

Four Trey and I sat up. We looked at each other, and grinned. His lips moved in speech, but of course I couldn't hear what he was saying. Then I spoke to him and neither of us could hear what I said.

We laughed; so relieved, you know. Just glad we weren't dead. He put a finger in his ear and wiggled it, then spoke to me again. His voice seeming to come to me from a thousand miles away.

". . . didn't hear you, Tommy. What did you say?"

"I just said," I said, carefully mouthing the words, "that it looks like we're still alive."

"Well, you'd just better be!" Carol sat down next to me. "I've got plans for you, Mr. Tommy Burwell."

The smoke and fumes of the dynamite were gone, and the air was sweet again. It was good to be there, with the peaceful night sounds all around us; the three of us sitting in the night on the Far West Texas prairie. And with all the excitement we'd been through, we needed to rest.

Carol sighed and snuggled close to me. Four Trey yawned and stretched, then crimped up his hat brim front and back. He kept looking away toward the trail to town, as though he were expecting something from that direction. And I finally asked him if he thought the gang would be back.

He drawled that he didn't think so. In fact, he was pretty sure that they wouldn't be.

"It's too bad they got away," I said. "I guess I didn't handle things very well."

"Now, don't you fault yourself, Tommy," he said. "You did just fine, and I'm proud of you."

I thanked him for his opinion, adding that I still hated it that they'd got away. "Maybe we could go over to camp and get one of the trucks or pickups started. If we could make it into town to a phone. . . ."

"We'd never do it, Tommy." He shook his head firmly. "Those flatbeds and pickups are knocked out for the next twelve hours, and you can bet money on it."

"Well. . . ." I looked at him frowning, thinking he was taking things pretty calmly. "It seems kind of strange that two men will be killed, two drivers, and that a month's payroll will be stolen without us doing a thing to stop it."

He shrugged, not saying anything, and continued to stare into the distance toward the trail to town. A moment or two passed, and then he asked me if I thought he'd made a mistake in not killing the Longs and everyone in their gang.

"They were right about that, you know. I had intended to kill 'em all. But when it came time to do it. . . ." He shook his head. "I just wasn't up to it, Tommy. I felt that they had to be given a chance to turn themselves in."

"Well," I said, "I guess I can understand that, all right. I know I couldn't just massacre a dozen men, no matter who they were. But. . . ."

"Exactly," he cut in. "Murder is murder, and I'd be as bad as they were. But if I gave them a chance and they didn't take it, then whatever happened to them would be their own doing."

"Yeah?" I hesitated. "How do you mean, whatever happened to them?"

"Well . . ." His shoulders moved again in a lazy shrug. "I was thinking that they might have an accident."

"Accident?"

"Why not? People have 'em on a lot better roads than that trail over there. And they're not driving with their lights off like Longie does."

"Well, yeah. But. . . ."

"Now, suppose something got dropped over there on the trail. Maybe kind of buried so that it was almost impossible to see. Longie would smash right into it, wouldn't he?"

"I guess so," I said. "But. . . ."

228

That was all I said. Because the whole sky suddenly lit up for miles around. A great blinding flash that turned the prairie night into day. Then came the explosion, the blast, and the ground trembled under us. And I was deafened for the second time that night.

Darkness returned. The echoes of the explosion died away. I rubbed my ears, shooting a glance at Four Trey.

"Well," I said. "I guess Longie hit something, all right."

"I guess he did," Four Trey said.